G000141601

CERTAIN VOICES

CERTAIN VOICES
Short stories about gay men

edited by
Darryl Pilcher

Boston: Alyson Publications, Inc.

Copyright © 1991 by Alyson Publications, Inc.
Cover design copyright © 1991 by Catherine Hopkins.
All rights reserved.

Typeset and printed in the United States of America.

This is a paperback original from Alyson Publications, Inc.
40 Plympton St., Boston, Mass. 02118.
Distributed in England by GMP Publishers,
P.O. Box 247, London N17 9QR England.

This book is printed on recycled paper.

First edition, first printing: June 1991

5 4 3 2 1

ISBN 1-55583-194-X

Contents

In memory of Paul Farmer

✳

Introduction

In the early spring of 1989, Alyson Publications began advertising nationwide for submissions for an anthology of gay male short fiction. The response was overwhelming, with nearly three hundred manuscripts received by the July 31 deadline. As editor of the project, only as I began reading through the nearly waist-high pile of stories did I realize just how difficult the decision-making process was going to be.

This collection was originally conceived as a follow-up to *Shadows Of Love*, the short-fiction anthology Alyson had published to great acclaim the year before. That book was distinguished by the fact that it featured writing from outside the metropolitan axis of New York–San Francisco–Los Angeles, giving gay writers in rural areas an opportunity to have their voices heard. However, as the number of manuscripts slowly whittled down, and the book began to assume a character of its own, the idea of an actual sequel seemed inappropriate. And while I certainly wanted to showcase new writers, some well-known authors slipped through the cracks with stories too fine to ignore.

After months of deliberation, I finally had the eighteen selections that comprise this volume. The criterion for my final decisions was simple: I chose the stories that compelled me to return to them again and again. These are the certain voices that refused to leave my head, thus providing me with a title as well.

The men you will meet in these pages span a lifetime of gay experience, from the rural Kansas teenager in Lucas Dedrick's "Burnt Things," whose destructive act of homophobia unearths a shattering revelation about his own sexuality, to the sixtyish Vatican priest seeking deliverance from a spiritual crisis through an S/M encounter in John Barrow's "Father Marcel."

AIDS and its ramifications are addressed in five stories: in the elegant prose of "I Am Here Now I Am Gone," Thomas Losito draws a poignant triangle between a PWA, his lover, and a handsome stranger; Jameson Currier's "Reunions" finds two survivors of a New York social circle fondly reminiscing about friends they've lost; the protagonist of Ron Woewoda's "Still the Night" journeys to a monastery in the Middle East for spiritual healing and has some wild adventures with the native men; Virginia Witt's "The Angel of Death on the Provincetown Ferry" features a healthy narcissist whose summer vacation takes an unexpected turn when he encounters a former lover stricken by AIDS; and in Michael Nava's "Grief," a surviving lover learns to set aside his pain and guilt and begin his life again.

There are also stories here that reflect diverse attitudes about our families, both biologic and chosen. "Bisonic Ballet (Pas de Deux)" is Robert Friedman's charming tale of the relationship between a man and his lesbian housemate's precocious young daughter, and Patrick Hoctel's "Families at Christmas" counterpoints a gay and lesbian household's bonding at the holidays with the protagonist's family's less-than-joyous Noel by long distance. Both stories are set in San Francisco, but that seems beside the point; they reflect our common need to plant a family tree from the seeds of friendship. And in a different kind of family story, Carter Wilson examines the powerful bond between a gay couple and their dogs in "The Day Dick Died."

Growing up gay and black is the subject of two very different, yet equally affecting stories. Randy Boyd's seething, powerful "Hostage" also touches on issues of AIDS and homophobia, while Larry Duplechan's "Presently in the Past" is a bittersweet childhood memoir about learning the painful lesson of being different. There are more surprises, but these I will leave for you to discover for yourself. I hope that everyone who picks up this book will find within its pages a piece of themselves.

I would like to acknowledge my debt of gratitude to Sasha Alyson for providing this rewarding opportunity. The wonderful staff of Alyson Publications provided endless support, especially Tina Portillo, who was my touchstone throughout this project. I'd like to thank Jeffrey McMahan for his second sight; Catherine Hopkins for a cover design that made my heart soar when I first saw it; manuscript readers Matthew Martin, Roger Seamans, Jim O'Loughlin, and Raymond Gamache; Wayne Curtis for his invaluable advice; and, especially, thanks to John Spellman for everything.

Darryl Pilcher
April 1991

Michael Schwartz · Public display

Stephen took another bite of his Quarter Pounder (with cheese), and let images from the McDonald's commercials gambol through his mind: boy meeting girl, grandparents spoiling grandkids, the nuclear family eating nuclear food, images all shiny-bright and squeaky with normality. Stephen was happy, lapped in the warm waters of irony. My God, he thought, it's wonderful how easy it is to be subversive when you're gay. Just do something that all the normal people do — like eat at McDonald's, or make love — but do it with a man. You feel like you're undermining society.

Stephen looked across the table at John, who was scowling at his Filet-O'-Fish sandwich. They were both more or less vegetarian (John more, Stephen less), and the fish was marginally less objectionable than the other non-beef entree, the Chicken McNuggets. Poor John, Stephen thought. But that's what he gets for treating this as food, instead of a socio-politico-esthetic field trip. Still, he was grateful that John would occasionally relax his standards and indulge

11

him in these ironic excursions. "You know I can't help myself," Stephen would explain.

"I know, you've told me," John would answer. "You're from New Jersey."

"Right. It's like a vampire, when he has to carry some of his native soil in his coffin, so he can sleep on it. Every so often, I have to touch trash, or I die."

John abandoned his sandwich, and focused instead on the conversation. It had actually been running for days, because he was trying to solve a problem at work. "I just have to tell my boss that I can't agree to a schedule that I know is impossible."

"Are you going to get blamed for making the project late?"

"No," John answered. "Everybody knows that Jim is going to be a month late with his part, and that gives me more than enough time to finish."

"So why doesn't Jim make a more realistic schedule?" Stephen already knew the answer, from previous conversations, but he also knew his role in this exchange. He was to ask the questions that would help John figure out what he had to do.

"Because," John said, exasperated, "because they all have this macho attitude, this refusal to admit any weakness, and that means we all have to promise what we can't deliver, and we can't even question what anyone else—"

He stopped, and they both turned to look at a nearby table, where a man and two boys were sitting. Then they looked back at each other.

"It was him, right?" John asked.

"Yes," Stephen answered, disgusted. "Why do they have to do this?"

"Was he talking about us?"

"I don't think so. I'm pretty sure he used the singular — 'that goddamn faggot.' If he meant us, he'd probably say 'those goddamn faggots.' Or maybe 'them there goddamn faggots.'"

John was intent on trying to hear. "Is he still saying it?"

Stephen looked at them again. The man was in his midthirties, about their own age. He wore a tight white polo shirt — his leisure clothes for this Saturday outing — and had a powerful build, which was obviously acquired on the job, not in the gym. He was balding, and his face was apoplectically red, as if always ready to explode. His two sons, both around ten, were thin and blond. They sat quietly, as if cowed by the anger in their father's voice, even though it wasn't directed against them.

"No," Stephen answered, after listening for a while. "The thing about the faggot was just a one-shot deal. Now he's complaining about the unions ... or maybe it's the Japanese ... whatever it is, he's against it."

John was visibly shaken. "This has never happened to me before."

"You've never heard anybody say 'faggot'?"

"Of course, but they usually yell it at you from a car, and then they speed away, like they know they're doing something wrong."

"Right. Then you give them the finger, and you hope they see it in the rearview mirror, and then you hope they don't turn around and come back and kill you."

"But this guy..." John looked at him again. "He's not running. He's just sitting there. He thinks he can just say it, and nobody will do anything about it."

"He's a straight white male. Nobody's told him yet that he doesn't own the world. It's probably because he does own it."

"Stephen, he can't get away with this."

"Oh, but he can. The Supreme Court said so: five-to-four decision."

"We've got to confront him."

"John..."

"What could happen? If we go over to him, and say, 'Excuse me'—"

"'Excuse me'?" Stephen echoed. "*That*'ll have him quaking in his boots."

"Okay," John laughed. "We'll work on the wording later." The laugh snapped John out of his initial shock, as Stephen had hoped. "But if we tell him that we're gay, and that what he said is offensive, what would he do?"

"Well," Stephen said, studying the man, "there's a chance — a slight chance — he'd say," Stephen dropped a half-octave, "'Gentlemen, I'd like to thank you for showing me the error of my ways. I'll never make a homophobic comment again. And, by the way, I want to thank you in particular for humiliating me in front of my sons.'"

"A chance. You think so?"

"I said 'a slight chance.' There's a slightly better chance that he'll scream, 'Faggots! They're gonna give my kids AIDS!' And then everyone will form a circle around us and stone us to death with Chicken McNuggets."

"Well," John mused, "martyrdom has always had its appeal."

"Actually," Stephen said, "what would probably happen is that you'd initiate a dialogue, and he'd start talking about how it's a free country and he has the right to say anything he wants, and how the family is threatened and do we want to wind up like the Roman Empire, and how God would have created Adam and Bruce, *et cetera*. And you'd be rational while he was being stupid. And he'd get annoyed, and you'd stay patient, and I'd get morose, and I'd probably have to kill both of you right there, just to get away."

John pretended to ponder. "I see. Well, if that's the worst, then I don't see any problem." Stephen flared his eyebrows at John, who quickly said, "Just joking! But seriously..."

Stephen interrupted. "I am serious."

14

"I know," John said. "But seriously. I know you think we can't do anything to educate him. But those kids — we can't let them think it's all right to call somebody a faggot."

"Oh," Stephen said, "they probably saw that afterschool special. You know, the one about the quiet, sensitive boy in class, and how you're not supposed to make fun of him, even if he does throw like a girl."

"That's not enough. They have to see it in real life, too. Stephen, we can't just sit here. We've got to do something."

Stephen knew John would say this. John had said it before.

These were in fact the first words that Stephen had ever heard John say. It was at a party, one of those early-evening parties where the point is moderate drinking and immoderate conversation. Stephen was walking toward the kitchen, the party around him a pleasant hum of amusing comments and amused laughter, when he became aware of a voice, distinct, cutting through the noise, saying, "But we've got to do something!" The speaker's urgency and earnestness were so out of place that Stephen was instantly alert to them.

Stephen saw the speaker, who was still addressing his audience of four listeners. Stephen didn't know him, but he knew he would. It wasn't just the prominent nose, the strong chin, the hairline beginning to recede over the temples — those physical traits that Stephen found so devastating. It had more to do with the way the man leaned forward into his explanation, his eyes alive with boyish enthusiasm and adult intelligence, his brow furrowed in concentration and concern. It was also the fact that, intent on his argument, the man had no idea that his audience was totally bored.

The man's lack of awareness made him seem absurd, vulnerable, and, to Stephen, heroic and beautiful. He wanted to rescue him, to protect him, to listen to him as he deserved to be listened to, to put his arms around him and fuck him and hold him all night long. He knew they'd sleep together that night: his desire was too precise to be wrong.

So Stephen joined the group, and picked up half the conversation, which was about the imminent demise of yet another gay rights bill. Stephen addressed the political issues, but with a wit and irony that wrapped themselves snugly around the other man's earnestness. The previously bored audience became attentive again, not so much to the political subject as to the sexual dynamic that was blossoming between the two speakers.

Stephen had been right. He charmed the pants off John that night — literally. What he hadn't foreseen was that, more than three years later, they'd still be together.

People who knew them declared the match inevitable, in retrospect, because they were both so serious about politics. And these people were right, up to a point. For both of them, growing up had been equal parts Mickey Mouse and Martin Luther King, the Fabulous Four and the Chicago Seven, Gloria Gaynor and Gloria Steinem — civil rights, antiwar, feminism. And, for both, these movements had served as rehearsals, preparations, for the central political action of their lives, which was also the most personal: accepting themselves as gay, and affirming that their life was worth living, and was worth protecting. For both, to be gay was to be political, because they saw the enormous power wielded by people who at best pitied them and at worst would be happy to see them dead. They took politics seriously — the way you would take a boulder seriously if it was perched on a cliff above your house.

But there were differences within this similarity; in the early seventies, Stephen had lost faith in public demonstrations — that article of belief so central to the creed of the sixties. In high school and college, he had marched against the war. He felt his single strength multiplied to infinity by the crowd of demonstrators; he saw himself as part of a force for historical change. But, when the war was over, and he watched the television footage of the last American helicopters leaving Saigon, he had a terrible realization: the protesters hadn't ended the war. Nixon and Kissinger had, when it suited their purposes to do so. Stephen never forgave them for that. In that moment, the sixties ended for Stephen, and the old Phil Ochs anthem took on a new meaning: "I ain't a-marchin' anymore."

Stephen remained political, but with a severely reduced sense of what an individual, or even a group of individuals, could accomplish when up against the mass of idiocy that democracy had endowed with power. His new creed was simple: you get involved in local politics, because you can have some impact. You vote Democratic in national elections, because you have no other choice. You give money to the ACLU, because court decisions matter. You maintain a supple sense of irony, because you're going to need it. And you live your life righteously, because anything else is death. Stephen made sure that everyone he touched directly — friends, colleagues, family, doctors, the clerks in the local convenience store — that they all knew he was gay, so that, if they had to vote on gay issues, they could picture an individual, rather than the child molester in drag pictured in homophobic propaganda. From an accumulation of these small actions, social change would come. Eventually. Maybe.

But he had no more illusions about educating the masses through public demonstrations and the like. To be educated, the masses needed to be capable of rational thought; and too many Republican administrations had proved that the masses would rather die than think. Instead of thought, they had tropisms, amoeboid movements prompted by primitive appetites and fears far beneath the reach of reason.

So these public demonstrations, these symbolic actions, these marches, rallies, and civil disobediences — they were worthless, and worse than worthless. They encouraged the participants to believe they were accomplishing something, when in fact they were doing nothing except making themselves feel good, which the current phrase-makers tried to ennoble by calling it "empowerment." It wasn't power; it was an opiate, no more. Better, Stephen maintained, to know that you can do nothing than to believe that your pathetic symbolic actions were accomplishing something. Better despair than delusion. Stephen didn't march, and he felt contempt for anyone who did.

John marched. He went to noontime rallies and all-night vigils; pro-union, anti-FDA, anti-antiabortion. He had been to every major Washington march since the massive antiwar demonstration in 1969. He had been arrested three times: nuclear power twice, and most recently at the Supreme Court. John marched because of the civil rights protests of the sixties. They had moved him, and educated him, and changed his life. Because he had been educated, he was generous enough to believe that others could be educated, too.

John's belief had a special fervor when it came to gay and lesbian issues, where standing up and being counted took on a literal meaning. Our invisibility, he argued, is our greatest enemy, and we must let the public know how many of us there really are. If tens or even hundreds of thousands of gays and lesbians poured into the streets, publicly demanding our rights, how, he reasoned, could we possibly be denied?

From the beginning, Stephen knew that John believed in the power of public demonstrations. Their first conversation was a debate on whether the many rallies for the gay rights bill were having any influence on public opinion. John said yes. Stephen said no. From that simple opposition, they launched into a sparring courtship. Each elaborated his views with wit and verve, spinning out more and more ingenious arguments, employing ever more hyperbolic rhetoric, drunk with words and ideas and desire, each trying to tease the other into yielding, each laughing at the other's stubbornness.

That night and afterwards, the charge between them transformed any differences into part of their erotic dance, elements in the interplay of irony and earnestness that formed their mutual attraction. When the topic of marching came up, it was as a contact point that was guaranteed to generate sparks. John would call Stephen a cynic, and Stephen would call John a sentimentalist, and the unresolved dispute would add a texture of tension to the way their bodies came together.

Then, one night a few months after they met, John asked Stephen where they should rendezvous the next day for the Gay Pride March.

Stephen was incredulous. "I don't march, John, you know that."

John laughed. "Oh, but, Stephen, couldn't you just come along? Think of it as taking a walk with me — and a couple thousand of my homosexual friends. It'll be cozy."

"You haven't been listening to me!"

"I know you say you don't march. But you were just being ironic, right? You weren't serious, were you?"

Stephen mustered all the earnestness that he was capable of. "I'm always serious. Irony is my way of being serious. I thought you understood that."

They were both silent, aware that something had changed between them. Until now, their conversation had been a joyous discovery of commonalities and complementaries. Some differences had of course turned up. John had been disappointed that Stephen didn't like *Hiroshima, Mon Amour;* Stephen had been appalled that John did. But those differences seemed peripheral — matters of taste, unlike this one, which came from deep within. It marked the first real limitation on what had, up to this point, seemed limitless.

19

Stephen looked at John — that nose and chin, those eyes, that hairline — who was sitting next to him, but who now seemed so separate. There is nothing, he thought, so alien as another human being. The difference between them suddenly felt like distance and, for the moment, the distance seemed unbridgeable. From that moment, his desire for John seemed pathetic, a doomed attempt to negate the distance. Bodies, beliefs, ideas — they're all barriers, not bridges: they mark a boundary that you can't go beyond; they keep you apart, even as you seem to be coming together.

Of course, the moment passed, and the common ground they had established outweighed the differences. Adjustments were made. The next day, John went to the Gay Pride March alone. His friends wondered at Stephen's absence and worried about a possible breach in this new and promising romance. But John just shrugged: "That's how Stephen is." There it was — a fact to be accepted.

Once, about a year later, they did try to domesticate the difference by turning it into an advantage. John was going to a Washington march, and they decided Stephen should go along. While John was marching, Stephen could go to the National Gallery. It didn't work. The separation during the day exaggerated the awareness of the difference between them. When they met for dinner that night, their talk trailed off into embarrassed silences, the kind that occurs at the reunion of two people who used to be friends. Since then, John would tell Stephen that he was going off to a march or protest, and Stephen would tell John to have a good time.

Stephen still believed that anyone who marched was a contemptible, self-deluded fool: major premise. He knew that John marched: minor premise. Ergo — but Stephen never finished the syllogism. For John's sake, Stephen acceded to a logical inconsistency in his inner world. There was too much of value between them, and a little disregard for the laws of logic seemed a small price to pay. Besides, this willed lapse in logic was probably what other people meant when they talked about love.

Anyway, the issue of public demonstrations came up only infrequently. It was certainly less visible than the standard relationship issues, like which holidays had to be spent with whose parents, and whether watching reruns of "Donna Reed" constituted sociological research. They didn't need to talk about demonstrations — except on occasions like this current one at McDonald's, when John felt that they had to "do something."

"Look," Stephen said, still trying to steer John away from a confrontation he knew would be pointless, at best. "It's too late to do anything now. There's a statute of limitations on responding to insults like this. You can't say, 'Sir, about that remark you made fifteen minutes ago'—"

"But, Stephen, if he's going to learn anything—"

"Exactly. It's like training a dog. If your dog shits on the rug, you've got to rub his nose in it right away. If you wait, he doesn't see the connection. It's the same with bigots. Except they're harder to train, because they're not as bright as dogs."

John frowned, deep in thought. Then he decided. "Well, we just have to make him say it again."

"What do you mean?" Stephen asked, apprehensively.

"We've got to provoke him into calling us 'faggots.'"

"I'm not sure it counts if we provoke him. It's entrapment, like a vice cop standing in a men's room pretending to be an available homosexual."

"Right." John agreed, warming to the argument. "It's time *we* tried that. And, besides, we're not pretending."

Stephen felt the discussion slipping out of his control. "But what do you want us to do?"

"Well," John answered, not quite sure, "we've got to do something that's ... you know, obviously gay."

"Like what?" Stephen demanded. "Hold a brunch? Start a fashion trend? How about my Bette Davis imita-

21

tion?" Stephen patted the side of his head. "'I'd love ta kiss ya, but I just washed my hair.'"

"That's it!" John cried.

"No, please, my Bette Davis is awful. How about my Jeanne Kirkpatrick?"

"No, I mean we could kiss."

Stephen was thunderstruck. "At McDonald's!" Even in his most subversive fantasies, he had never imagined this ultimate act of revolution.

"Sure," John insisted. He waved his hand, indicating the people around them. "They're doing it. We can, too."

"John. Look around. Nobody's kissing. It's McDonald's, for Christ's sake. Even straights have their limits."

"Okay," John conceded. "But they could kiss, if they wanted to, so they don't. We can't, so we have to."

Stephen felt outmaneuvered. This was exactly the kind of logic he understood. He shifted ground. "John," he said, a hint of mock pleading in his voice, "you're asking me to commit a PDA."

John was stumped. "Politically — Dysfunctional — Anachronism?"

"Public Display of Affection. In high school, senior year, we took a class trip to Washington. The principal lectured us on how we were representing our school, so we shouldn't commit any PDAs. Of course, I wasn't about to commit any. The only PDA I wanted to commit was on Jeff Samuels, and Michelle Czernak would have scratched my eyes out."

"The thing is," John said, "that they eventually get to commit their what-do-you-call-its, their PDAs. We don't. Our whole life is like high school, with everybody saying, 'Don't commit PDAs.'"

Stephen was silent, so John continued. "We've been together, what, three years?"

"Three and a half."

"And in all that time, have we ever committed a PDA?"

Stephen thought for a moment, then smiled. "Well there was that time on the night flight from California."

"That was not intended to be public! We were just lucky that the flight steward turned out to be ... uh..."

"Simpatico?" Stephen suggested.

"Yes." John smiled, and blushed at the memory. "My God, you're evil. The things you make me do! And you know that's not what I mean. I mean a time when we're affectionate in public, when other people, straights, strangers, can see ... you know, what we mean to each other."

Stephen threw his hands into the air. "I'm a WASP. We don't do PDAs. Even married WASPs just shake hands with each other. I think we procreate through our palms."

John motioned Stephen to be quiet. "No, there was that time last year when I had to go home for my uncle's funeral, and you drove me to the airport. You kissed me, right on the lips, at the security gate. You were so sweet. I was so surprised. It got me through the whole dismal weekend."

Stephen sank into glumness. "I was afraid you'd bring that up. Okay. I surrender. You're right."

"What do you mean?" John asked, perplexed.

Stephen sighed deeply, hung his head, and confessed. "All the way to the airport I was brooding about it, before I did it. I felt I had to do it, so I rehearsed it in my mind, over and over." He spoke with surprising bitterness. "It was totally preplanned. I kiss my grandmother with more passion."

John hesitated, then put his hand on Stephen's arm. "Don't be so hard on yourself. It's not easy."

Stephen looked up at John. "It never ends, does it? You keep finding new ways that they've fucked you up. And you keep fighting to unfuck it. Okay. Let's kiss. But this isn't only for that guy's benefit. I'm asserting my right to be publicly tacky, just like Jeff Samuels and Michelle Czernak."

"That's my boy!" John said.

They sat there, frozen.

Stephen moaned, "Why do I feel like an adolescent on his first date?"

"Okay," John said, giving himself a pep talk. "I've organized rallies with hundreds of people. I can organize this."

"Oh, great," Stephen muttered.

"Stephen! You agreed."

"Okay, it's your scene. So what do you want — a quick peck?"

"No," John answered, considering carefully. "It has to be a good long kiss. We need to make sure he sees it."

"Do you want sound effects? A nice, wet smack at the end?"

"No. Too adolescent. We want to project an image of maturity."

Stephen smiled slyly. "Can I slip you some tongue?"

"Absolutely not!" John reprimanded. "We want to be affectionate, not lewd. This is an assertion of our right to love. It's just a spontaneous expression of our affection for each other."

"This is about as spontaneous as brain surgery. I feel like a panda in a zoo, about to be mated. Maybe we should call the press in before—"

"Oh, no!" John was looking at the next table. Stephen looked, too. The man and his sons were leaving, preempting the little performance that was being so carefully prepared just for them.

They sat silent for a while. John was obviously disappointed at having missed his chance to make a public statement. Then he rallied himself. "Oh, well. At least we're ready for the next time. We'll know what to do when it happens again."

Stephen looked at John — his die-hard marcher, his brave little demonstrator, whose sixties gleam was still shining bright, even as the nineties were darkening around

24

them. In his enthusiasm for public encounters, John seemed as absurd as the first time Stephen had seen him, over three years ago, at the party — as absurd, and as beautiful. He knew he'd never convince John that his marching was pointless. And he was sure that he wanted to convince him. There would be this part of John that was forever beyond his reach.

Desire, Plato tells us, can be only for what we do not possess, because, since desire is the desire to possess, once we possess something, we can no longer desire it. By that definition, and by so many others, what Stephen felt for John at this moment was desire.

Stephen leaned across the table, and said, in a hoarse whisper, "Let's kiss anyway."

"What?" John was surprised, a little startled by Stephen's tone.

"You're so hot when you're being political."

John lowered his head, and blushed profoundly. "I still can't tell when you're being serious."

"I keep telling you. I'm always serious. Just kiss me. You'll see."

So they did, and John did see. So did everyone else. Most of them didn't like it, but that didn't matter. Because this was a private moment, that just happened to be occurring in a public place.

Patrick D. Hoctel
Families at Christmas

It was the first Christmas I hadn't gone home, and it was because of a fight. "Home" was where my parents lived in Harahan, Louisiana, the same ranch-style, three-bedroom, two-bath house they'd occupied for the last thirty-two years.

The fight was about money — my not having any. My parents were always offering me money when I didn't need it, but when, between teaching jobs, I suggested they buy my ticket home as my present, I was met with a stiff "We'll have to let you know."

There followed a letter from my mother decrying everything I'd done since high school, including growing a beard, getting a master's in English, and moving to the most expensive city in the country, San Francisco. The letter went on to say that my parents were getting older and were not a money tree.

We made up in our traditional manner — by pretending it never happened. When my parents asked why I wasn't spending the holidays with them, I replied that I was too busy working on my syllabus for the fourth quarter, a task

26

which took me all of an afternoon since I'd taught freshman composition for the past three years.

＊

I lived in a decidedly offbeat but politically correct neo-pagan lesbian and gay household whose attitude toward the Yuletide season was ambiguous at best. I'd moved into Harmony House in May. My housemates were friendly enough but suspicious. I was younger than they, I owned a television, and I occasionally ate meat in restaurants. But I did have a steady income, an Abyssinian cat they adored, and a willingness to listen to almost anything they had to say.

I thought they were strange, and they thought I wasn't strange enough, but we got on. The one I could never be sure of was Danforth, the unofficial head of the household and a terror. Danforth — no one ever called him Dan — had the heaviest tread of any human I'd ever encountered, and his morning trip to the shower sounded like the condemned going to the gallows. He also hated to be spoken to when he was eating or reading or about to eat or read and would answer all my too-polite, mundane pleasantries with nods, raised eyebrows, and poorly concealed sighs. Jhara, renamed from Dwayne, I never saw much. He was the most scheduled person I'd ever come across and late for every event, so he tended to come and go in a whirl of constant tardiness.

I spent most of my time in our rambling two-story Victorian on Divisadero with Sabina and her four-year-old son, Nathan. Sabina was a Jewish lesbian and a women's rights activist, and Nathan, partial product of the Oakland sperm bank, was her foul-mouthed towhead, who was nevertheless a pleasure to be around, even when he was screaming, "Come wipe my ass" when through on the toilet.

Sabina would steal into my room on Wednesday nights after Nathan was asleep and Danforth was downstairs

27

reading Barbara Tuchman or some such to watch "Dynasty" in the days when Alexis and her facsimiles ruled the Castro, t-shirts, greeting cards, and coffee cups. Sabina claimed it was her only sin, and I believed her. We screamed a lot, but I sensed a secret shame behind her laughter, as if the knowledge that she could be doing something truly useful with this time weighed on her.

※

Christmas morning dawned misty and gray after a tense Christmas Eve spent around Tillie, the potted pine we'd rolled in off the porch for our Christmas tree. Jhara had promised to be home that evening, and after we'd waited, then gone ahead and arranged Tillie in a corner of the living room, he'd burst through the door with three shopping bags full of ornaments.

Sabina found the red balls and twinkle lights objectionable on esthetic grounds — they *were* garish — and Danforth wasn't about to sanction angels or Santa and Mrs. Clauses for any tree he was decorating. He also wasn't impressed by my argument that the angels could be interpreted as muses or sprites, and Sabina came right out and said they were ugly. Our debate was capped by Nathan scooping dirt from Tillie's base and dumping it over his head while loudly proclaiming over and over, "I hate fucking Christmas."

Enfolded in my sheets while waiting for whichever housemate to finish in the bathroom, I tended to agree with Nathan and considered that my life was not turning out as I'd intended. I was zeroing in on thirty without a boyfriend, a job I liked, or even an invitation to a New Year's Eve party. Here I was in the gay mecca, and I might as well have been in Toledo.

A reflex reaction I knew better than to trust made me roll halfway off my futon and go for the phone. "You'll always have a home with us," one of my family's favorite refrains, tinkled brightly in my ears, and my fingers, still dull with sleep, jabbed out the long-distance number.

On the other end someone wordlessly picked up and waited for me to speak, a baby crying softly close by. "Your daughter's crying," my brother said finally.

"It's Paul," I said. "How are you?"

"Fine," my brother replied, not pleased at this case of mistaken identity. "Look, Mom's in the back." I heard him shout for her. My brother hated to talk on the phone; actually, he hated to talk, period. At eighteen or nineteen he had become monosyllabic like many straight men seem to and talking became a chore for him. Too many questions and he'd get up and leave a room, so I didn't ask what was wrong. Instead I listened to my three-month-old niece's tearful gurgles.

Suddenly Mom was on the line, telling someone near her in a tight voice that she'd understood what they'd said the first time. "Merry Christmas, honey," Mother said.

Unlike my brother, my mother needed little prompting to blurt out her troubles. The most innocent "How are things?" brought a torrent down on my head.

"Horrible," she said. "I've been locked in the bathroom all morning. Crying my eyes out."

Mother was not a crier, so I knew something major had happened. What Mother was, though, was a storyteller, one prone to embellishment.

"I can't talk," Mother went on, "but, needless to say, Christmas is ruined. I'll never forgive her for that, and not so much as one 'I'm sorry I ruined your Christmas, and I swear not to do it again.' Not one word. Nothing."

Mother did talk, however, and it turned out my sister-in-law had asked my brother for a divorce on Christmas Eve — right after the presents exchange — while staying in the room next to my parents'. When he'd refused, she'd fled to her parents, leaving him with the baby. Mother had locked herself in the bathroom, because every time she looked at her granddaughter, she broke into sobs, which upset the baby. "Be glad you didn't come home," she whispered before hanging up. I didn't argue.

✳

Downstairs was fairly festive. Tillie remained unadorned, but she was very green with the sun shining in on her and emitting a splendid odor. Jhara sat cross-legged by her side, stringing popcorn garlands, the one tree decoration we'd reached consensus on. Sabina and Nathan were busy cutting out snowflakes to hang along the fireplace mantle, which was already festooned with fir branches and holly. Danforth admitted going to Buena Vista Park early that morning and gathering them. "I felt a bit ridiculous after last night," he said. "I'm not the most flexible person, but I do try." On the stereo Joan Baez was singing in her silver-bell tones about the "Little Drummer Boy," and my *Phil Spector's Christmas Album* was next in line for the turntable.

"This isn't a big deal," Danforth announced from the kitchen, "but I'm making grilled cheese sandwiches with tomatoes for anyone who wants them. And for dessert," he paused — Danforth, like my mother, was no stranger to drama — "stewed quinces with hand-cranked ice cream."

We four in the living room cheered, perhaps a bit wildly, because Danforth stepped back toward the French doors and clasped his hands in front of him. "It's nice to be appreciated," he allowed.

After the grilled cheese sandwiches, which featured blackened crusts, the way Danforth liked them, we gathered in the front room. Inspired by Baez and the Ronettes, we'd agreed, rather spontaneously for us, to reclaim a few Christmas carols as our own. Grouped around the old upright piano, we stumbled through "Oh, Christmas Tree," "Deck the Halls," "Winter Wonderland," and "Frosty the Snowman." Secular but seasonal tunes, the last at Nathan's request.

30

The problem was that, without songbooks, we could only recall a few lines of each and had to hum the missing parts. Nathan quickly lost interest in this enterprise and left the room to stare at the booty stacked around Tillie. We adults made a last, valiant stab at "Silent Night," ignoring the obvious religious content, then tore into the gifts, righteously pleased with ourselves for remembering every word.

My gift from Sabina, greeted with bemused "Hmms" from Danforth and Jhara, was a year's subscription to *TV Guide*. A piece of flattened mistletoe marked the page where the first "Dynasty" of the new year had been highlighted with a yellow marker. Danforth gave me Jonathan Katz's *Gay American History* and the Matchbox edition of my dream car, the Jaguar XKE.

"You're encouraging bourgeois leanings," I told the two, and they smiled shamefacedly, happy that I was happy but guilty as charged. Jhara's present was to be forthcoming; he'd been too frantic to shop.

For Danforth I'd gotten a new biography of Marie of Romania. "You know me *too* well," he said when he spied her picture on the cover. Despite his progressive politics, he was something of a closet monarchist, but only when it came to his reading material.

For Sabina I'd scoured the city for a sheer black camisole, which drew approving whistles from the men. "I see I'm going to have to hide this," she muttered. After much urging she stood and held the camisole in front of her, modeling a little for our benefit. "I don't know," she said, studying herself in the mirror above the fireplace, "it's a different me."

"Another side of the total you," I ventured in my best commercial announcer's voice.

In the back room of the kitchen, the phone rang, and I ran to answer it. It was Mother calling to fill me in on the latest — my sister-in-law's return.

"A bad case of holiday jitters," Mother said. "An infant on her hands, plus her folks were jealous she and Tony and the baby were here. They're no prizes, those people."

During my mother's account of tragedy averted, the bell rang, and I heard a chorus of "Surprise!" at the front door. Five little boys of various shades and sizes spilled into the living room with Nathan in the lead. Our house was soon filled with Osh Kosh overalls, the sound of snaps unsnapping, and mothers reminding their sons not to leave their things all over the place, even as they stooped to pick them up.

"What's that racket?" Mother demanded.

"Kids," I said. "You always say, 'Christmas isn't Christmas without children in the house.'" I couldn't resist tossing one of my mother's hoary chestnuts back at her.

"I still believe that," Mother said slowly.

She was waiting for an explanation, but I didn't have the stamina to go into details about Sabina's natal group and the five lesbian mothers who'd all had boys because of something having to do with sperm temperature. "They're Nathan's friends," I said, which was the truth if not the whole truth, a lie of omission at worst.

From my perch on a stool, I watched Danforth in an armchair settle Nathan on his lap. The children hushed as Danforth began to read in an appropriately stentorian voice the fourth chapter, "Mr. Badger," of *Wind in the Willows*, Nathan's favorite book and character.

Mother and I talked on, my mind drifting in and out of her recitation of the day's events and my own private thoughts as Danforth intoned, "'Any friend of *mine* walks where he likes in this country, or I'll know the reason why!'" This from a man who a half hour and a large brandy earlier was doing an impersonation of Tallulah Bankhead as she drunkenly stumbled into a church during Christmas services and, her eyes coming to rest on a crucifix above the altar, raised her martini glass and exclaimed, "Happy birthday, dahling!"

"Everything's okay then," I said.

"I wouldn't go as far as that," Mother cautioned, "but we're all speaking."

The house was quiet but not still. Life vibrated through it as Danforth wound down the chapter.

...simultaneously they turned and made swiftly for home, for firelight and the familiar things it played on, for the voice, sounding cheerily outside their window, of the river that they knew and trusted in all its moods, that never made them afraid with any amazement.

As he hurried along, eagerly anticipating the moment when he would be at home again among the things he knew and liked, the Mole saw clearly that he was an animal of tilled field and hedgerow, linked to the ploughed furrow, the frequented pasture, the lane of evening lingerings, the cultivated garden plot. For others the asperities, the stubborn endurance, or the clash of actual conflict, that went with Nature in the rough; he must be wise, must keep to the pleasant places in which his lines were laid and which held adventure enough, in their way, to last for a lifetime.

Lev Raphael Another life

Send me out into another life
Lord because this one is growing faint
—W.S. Merwin
"Words from a Totem Animal"

Nat had not started coming to Michigan State's small Orthodox congregation two years ago to look for a man. He expected to feel safe there, hidden, because it was not like his parents' huge suburban synagogue outside Detroit — all gleaming polished oak, a theater, a social hall, a stage. In the Jewish Students' Center at the edge of campus, they prayed in a bare, high-ceilinged narrow room that was like an exercise in perspective, drawing your eyes inexorably to the plainly curtained Ark in front. His first time, he'd sat in the last row, on the men's side, alone, after putting on his prayer shawl and slipping a prayer book from the crowded chest-high bookcase behind him. At the small slanting-topped lectern, a man was praying aloud wrapped in an enormous black-barred wool prayer shawl as large as a flag. Nat's little polyester one, gold-embroidered like a sampler, seemed incongruous, almost ugly — though it was what he'd always used since his bar mitzvah. The man came back to shake Nat's hand at the point where waiting for enough men to continue with prayers began, and got Nat's Hebrew name for when he would call him to the lectern. Nat always regretted just being a *Yisroel*, one of the vast majority of Jewish men. *Levis* claimed descent from the Temple functionaries who sang the psalms and were entitled now to the second Torah blessing at services. *Cohens* were descended from the priests and had the first Torah blessing in synagogues; Nat liked this remnant of the Temple hierarchy even though he was at the bottom (his sister, Brenda, said, "Well, then, that leaves *me* underground!").

Only six of the thin-seated black-plastic-and-chrome chairs were filled that first morning, by guys who would have been unexceptional on campus or in town but here looked costumed and exotic in prayer shawls and skullcaps. They all chatted for a while. Most were graduate students, but for Nat they had the authority of much older men, because of their deep Jewish knowledge and the way they prayed.

The few women — wives, a girlfriend — were pale, plain, undemanding. Nat was glad they were on the other side of the six-foot-high wooden barrier — the *mehitzah* — separate, even after services, even talking to the men, still as private and inaccessible as ducks brooding by the river on campus. They came to consider him shy, he knew, because he seldom initiated a conversation.

Nat had always watched other men pose, lean, grin, and entertain women, as if from a distance, thinking they looked like clownishly intense animals in mating desperation, all puffed up on display. Nat couldn't mimic the flattery and ogling, because women had never stirred a desire even to pretend in him. They were merely figures in a landscape.

The Orthodox service on Saturday mornings was very long, almost four hours, and some of the prayers and melodies were unfamiliar at first, but the direction and sequence was similar to the services he'd grown up with, and coming every week, he began to fit inside this new structure for belief. Nat's Hebrew, always better than Brenda and his parents knew, blossomed until he felt confident enough to offer to do part of the service. It was such a small congregation, usually less than fifteen except on holidays, that praying here was intensely private for him, thankfully not a time to see relatives or friends from high school, or be shown off by his parents as a faithful son. Sometimes he was so moved, he covered his head with the new, large prayer shawl he'd bought in Southfield, shutting the world and everyone out as the truly Orthodox did.

The singing, the absence of English, the spiritual concentration — *kavannah* — seemed beautiful to him, as if they were all, at the most powerful moments, the fabulous gold cherubim on the Ark of the Covenant, over which hovered God's presence. Sometimes he felt *that* holy, *that* moved beyond himself — but whom could he tell? The few Jewish acquaintances he had at State weren't interested in hearing about his discoveries. Most people would just classify him as a fanatic, like his parents seemed to (Brenda listened, but not with enthusiasm), and even the congregation's regulars stayed away from talking about feelings or anything verging on mysticism. For them, the service was simply the right and only way to pray.

Yet he welcomed their self-absorption. He had really come here, at first, before he was seduced by the service itself, hoping that the Orthodox congregation, the *minyan*, might be a bath of acid in which he could burn away like verdigris from bronze his obsessions about men. He'd heard about druggy friends saved by joining Orthodox communities in Brooklyn, and lazy and almost criminal "trouble" students at his high school straightening out in Hasidic enclaves of Jerusalem, and had hoped for a similar miracle. Nothing else had worked.

Acting had not helped him lose himself, but brought him into a terrifying world of men who blared their availability and were always making reconnaissance raids on guys who didn't. Learning French and starting on Russian had only given him new words, not a new identity. Running did make him fit, and supplied a hobby and completely new range of conversation — shoes, tracks, breathing, diet, shin splints, marathons, stars, books, and magazines — but he was still only Nat for all those miles. And he only admired other runners more, became a connoisseur of those wonderful high round asses, those long and heavy thighs. When he watched track-and-field events on TV, he waited for close-ups or slow-motion shots to see the heavy weight inside a favorite runner's thin and clinging shorts whip and swing from thigh to thigh.

Even at services, alone with the other men, trying to stay deep in prayer, his thoughts sometimes wandered: to a barefoot guy in cutoffs hosing down his car across the street, who'd glanced at him one morning as Nat entered the building; or two wide-backed, tanned bikers damp with sweat and exhaustion shouting to each other as they cut down the street; or even Italian-looking Clark, who helped run the *minyan*, Clark whose weight lifting had left him as bulging and tight as a tufted leather sofa. Nat's private gallery. He felt then lonelier than ever, tracing the path of his unquenched thirst for men, to be a man (was that different? the same?), back to childhood. When had he not felt this way? And what would it be like never to look at men but only *see* them: pure registration without excitement, interest, pain? He was always feeling helpless, like turning a corner in town to almost bump into a guy in sweatpants with those seductive gray folds, whose belly seemed harder, flatter over the shifting jock-rounded crotch, or watching someone's tight jutting ass in the locker room at the gym as he bent over to pull up his shorts.

Still he could lose himself in prayer often enough, long enough. And then his sister, Brenda, doing her Ph.D. at State, began to join him at services after he'd learned the cantillation for reading the Torah. With her, he felt more anchored, sure this might be an answer if only he waited. Brenda wasn't pleased with sitting on the women's side at first, but she respected what he'd learned, or at least all the weeks of practicing at her apartment with a tape recording, chanting to himself there because it drove neighbors at the dorm crazy. And *he* was pleased that his pretty sister drew attention from the men, as if her presence made him less of a shadow or a blank, less suspiciously alone. With Brenda at services he felt he could be normal — or seem that way — and sometimes it was easier to concentrate. Thoughts of men were not so intense; she was like a powerful signal jamming pirate broadcasts.

"I didn't think I would, but I like the service," she admitted after a few months. "I don't even mind the *mehitzah* anymore. I don't get distracted looking around, like back home."

At men, he thought, wondering what she had guessed about him.

Perhaps she knew everything and didn't want to mention it, like the Jews in polls done by national Jewish magazines who overwhelmingly supported civil rights for homosexuals, but didn't want to have to see what that meant in their own lives. This unspoken demand for invisibility was more enlightened than Judaism's traditional distaste for homosexuality, but Nat could not find the difference very comforting.

❋

Nat watched Mark's strong shoulders inside the black-striped prayer shawl on Mark's first *shabbos* at the Orthodox congregation. Mark read Torah with a slow persuasive rise and fall, beautiful large hands flat on the lectern, rocking softly, and Nat found himself staring at his smooth thick lips when Mark brought the Torah around and he touched this prayer book to the velvet-sheathed scroll. Mark nodded.

Mark was a Levi, and Nat imagined him in the Jerusalem Temple, strong feet bare, curly hair and beard fragrantly oiled. With those deep-set blue eyes and beard growing high on his cheeks, and the muscular frame, he looked distant, romantic, like someone's burly wild grandfather in an old photograph: a man who had disappeared on an adventure in Australia or Brazil. Nat drank and drank Mark's every movement on that criminally hot and dusty June *shabbos* Mark first came to services. When Mark kissed his prayer book on closing it, or bowed during certain prayers, the gestures were smooth and authentic expressions of a certainty Nat found seductive, and that made Mark unlike anyone else he knew.

In the little crowd after services, they discussed Mark's doing part of the service next week. Mark talked briefly about having just taken an administrative job at State, after a similar position at NYU, and Nat told him about being raised Reform. He described their invisible choir and organ, the three gowned rabbis who had seemed like Hollywood extras, watching them high on their stage from a sharply raked auditorium. It was theater to him back then, distant and boring.

Mark smiled. "So how'd you wind up here?"

Nat hesitated.

And Mark invited him back for *shabbos* lunch after they chatted with Brenda, who assured Mark she had other plans.

They walked the mile or so from the Jewish Center in an almost incandescent heat — even Nat's skullcap seemed too warm and heavy.

Nat did most of the talking, and felt very young again, excited, as if he were on the verge of a birthday present or a longed-for trip.

The air conditioning had left Mark's place blissfully cold. "This is just temporary," Mark said, explaining the boxes all over his featureless apartment. "I'm looking for somewhere nice."

39

They set the table, and Nat tried not to falter when he handed Mark the silver laver at the sink after washing his hands and drying them while saying the blessing. Sitting opposite Mark, Nat watched him say *Hamotzi* — the prayer over bread — long hands on the swelling shiny challah. Mark sliced a piece, salted it, and gave Nat half.

"This is beautiful." Nat fingered the linen cloth, the silver.

"Wedding presents." And then he shrugged. "That was a long time ago — it's not important."

After lunch of a traditional *shabbos* cholent — the meat-and-beans stew that baked overnight — and singing the prayers, they played Scrabble and read the Detroit newspapers in a silence so comfortable Nat felt as purified and free as after an hour in the campus steamroom.

"Why don't you stay?" Mark said near six o'clock.

"For dinner?"

Mark smiled and slipped off his skullcap, then shook his head.

"Stay with *me*. Aren't you gay?"

Eyes down, Nat said, "I've never done this."

"But don't you want to?" Mark came to hold him tightly, stroking his hair, his arms and face, taming the wild beast fear, and then led him into the bedroom. Mark stripped. His body was statue-hard, blazingly dark and public — as if all the men Nat had ever gawked at padding from the showers to their lockers; or lifting weights, shoulders and face bulging as if to hurl themselves up through the roof; or lounging near the pool in bathing suits no larger than index cards — as if their essence had been focused like a saving beam of light into this room, for him.

He pulled off his clothes and moved to hug Mark, entering that light which seemed now to blaze up inside of him as he rubbed himself against Mark.

"Wait."

Mark led him close to the mirror on the closet door, slipped behind him. "Look. *Look.*" With one hand he held Nat's head up so that Nat was forced to see his own wide eyes, and Mark's guiding him. He leaned back into Mark as if cushioned by water in a heated pool, floating, hot, abandoned, as Mark lightly ran fingers along his sides, down to his thighs, and back up, circling, teasing, calling up sensations from his skin like a wizard marshaling a magical army from dust and bones. Nat watched his body leap and respond as if it, too, were urging him to keep his eyes open and unashamed. Mark slipped one dark and hairy hand down from his waist to grasp him; the other stroked his chest. Mark kissed his neck, his ears, his hair.

"Don't look away."

The words came to Nat as if in a dream in which he was a solitary tourist lost in some vast but familiar monument whose history and meaning he strained to understand in a shower of pamphlets. He struggled, he gave in, staring into Mark's eyes watching *him* watch an incomprehensible act that ended — for now — with a savage rush as he came, and Mark grinned, laughed, right hand wet and white.

Later that night they took a walk to campus, and it was a bit cooler where they sat by the river.

"Sometimes I feel transported, completely," Mark told him, explaining why he was often intoxicated by *davening* — prayer. "On *Rosh Hashonah* once I saw my shadow on the wall in *shul, yarmulkah,* beard, and it didn't look like me. It could've been anyone, any Jew, who knows where, how far back."

Ducks, white and startling in the dark, idled against the river's current. Nat breathed in the faint sweetness of Mark's skin and hair, wanting to brush a hand in his beard.

"You know," Mark began, "there's a legend that Torah is written in letters of black fire on white fire. Sometimes I can almost see it."

Nat admired how for Mark being Jewish was home, not a foreign land to be approached with guidebooks and a map.

He thought about black and white fire the next *shabbos,* and found himself crying when they sang "Av Harachamin," Compassionate Father, before the Torah was taken out of the Ark, their voices blended and thoughtful, not loud as usual. As Mark's soulful voice rose above the others, Nat felt open and faint, wanting to rise, enter, disappear.

When Mark blessed the wine after services, he was beautiful in his brown slacks and beige shirt and brown-and-beige Italian silk tie, not at all like the other guys in the *minyan,* whose shabbiness was almost boastful.

"Are you okay?" Brenda asked Nat. "Are you getting a cold or something?" She was their family's smart one and the beauty — slim-hipped, gray-eyed, magnetic in a bikini, with curly long almost-red hair, face wide and kind and striking, with Dad's strength and Mom's charm — but Nat no longer felt like her tagalong, plain, and unimpressive little brother.

"I'm great," he said.

Nat helped Mark move to a larger apartment farther from town. It was splendidly cool, neutral-toned, all gleaming glass and brass, a construction perfect and complete. And with its balcony view of a man-made lake, it was like a brand-new eraser wiping Nat's ugly dorm room from a board like a hopelessly misspelled sentence. He hated leaving Mark's place, which felt like his first real home.

At the dorm he had to laugh at the jokes about getting laid, about faggots, had to be careful not to stare at anyone getting out of the shower or even stare into the mirror at the reflection of someone half-dressed, or nude under an open robe, shaving, spitting, scratching, praying for consciousness. Here he felt safe, could shower with Mark, stroke his back, go nude, bite Mark's ass in the kitchen, be completely free, or at least grow toward that freedom, and no one knew. Even when they just went out for dinner, or to a movie, he was not relaxed. He felt stared at, wondering if they looked like more than friends.

Mark insisted that here in a college town it was different than in New York; most people wouldn't assume two men together were *together:* "Look at all those jocks, and the fraternities." But Nat disagreed, worried about the ten years between them, wishing that he too were big, broad, and dark, bearded, blue-eyed, hairy, so that they could look like brothers or cousins.

Nat's fear led to their first explosion. Mark had bought them expensive seats for an upcoming Chicago Symphony performance on campus — an all-Russian program of Ruslan and Ludmilla, *Sacre de Printemps,* and Prokofiev's Fifth Piano Concerto. But Nat just set aside the card with the tickets and didn't smile at his surprise that came with dessert.

"That's a *date,*" he said. "Everyone will see us."

Mark was silent after that, rinsing off the dinner dishes in their sink of soapy water, starting the dryer, wiping the counter. He hung up the dish towel, his movements heavy, admonishing.

Nat sat at the table, waiting out the silence, feeling as if he'd entered a room of celebration with news of someone's death — important but guilty.

Leaning back against the sink, thick arms crossed, not even looking at him, Mark almost spat out, "What is *wrong* with you? Why is everything so fucking secret? You won't even tell your *sister* about us!"

"We're not in New York, this is Michigan, and we're Jewish, and it's wrong."

"Sure! And tell me you voted for Reagan! Is it wrong for *you,* does it make you a monster? Will you stop lighting candles, stop being a Jew?"

"Sometimes at services I feel like I shouldn't *be* there, shouldn't kiss the Torah or do anything."

"That's what your *parents* would say, your *rabbi*, not you! You don't believe that, you *can't*. When are you going to stop *hating* yourself?"

Mark went on, and Nat hardly listened, but he felt the passion in Mark's voice and felt near tears, wishing Mark's message of acceptance was not like the anguished cry of someone aboard a ship that was pulling out to sea calling back to the dock, "Jump in, hurry, *swim!*"

And then he *was* crying, and Mark handed him a napkin and said, "Oh, *fuck* the concert."

"No," Nat said. "Fuck *me*." When Mark had first wanted to fuck him on their first night together a month before, Nat had pulled away as if slapped. It seemed impossible — too brutal and strange, and painful proof of how far he would have traveled from his incoherent fantasies of being with a man. He said no then, and had kept saying it, but now his fear of what it meant, what it would feel like, fell from him in a rush, like the fan-shaped leaves of his parents' gingko tree, which could drop in one cool fall day. He smiled. "Fuck *me*."

With Mark's weight around and inside him, Nat felt like all those characters he'd never understood in *The Rainbow* and *Women in Love* — annihilated by sex, transformed beyond words.

When Mark was finally asleep, Nat imagined his parents bursting in on them, Brenda horrified, old friends nodding, "Sure, I always knew." What could he tell them?

It was oddly like the first time he had prostrated himself on *Yom Kippur* at the Orthodox services during the service of the High Priest, the only time Jews ever did that in prayer. The service described in lavish detail the High Priest's preparation for entering the Holy of Holies and everyone, many *thousands* of people at the Temple mount, throwing themselves to the ground when the Priest pronounced the Name of God in a way lost to history and the multitude crying, "Praised be His glorious sovereignty throughout all time! — *Baruch shem kavod malkuto layolom vaed.*" With his forehead touching the floor, tired, hungry from fasting, intent, awed by the moment kept intact through two thousand years, Nat had known that his final, unexpected willingness to surrender to something beyond his understanding was a border, a crossing that would always mark him as different from what he had been.

John Barrow — **F**ather Marcel

F ather Marcel, en route from Rome to Cincinnati, sank
back into the roomy comfort of his first-class seat on the
Alitalia 747, picked up the letter from Lee Horne, and
opened it, reminding himself that he really must arrange a
visit between them the next time he was in New York. This
Roman Catholic monk, in his occupation as supervisor for
certain English-speaking orders throughout the world, frequently passed through New York. Every four years he was
obliged to check up on their house on the Hudson River;
more often he was in the city for the purpose of taking large
amounts of money from wealthy benefactors to further the
aims of his order — useful aims — seminaries in India,
orphanages in Korea.

It was worthwhile work; the visits to the estates of the
rich were pleasant, the food good; the money was badly
needed by his order; and Father Marcel was adept at
separating it from his patrons. People with money seemed
to like his jolly mood and his sincerity, and to be puzzled
by his penetrating wit. He was short of stature, with a
creamy face lit up by bright blue eyes. A band of cropped

silver hair crowned his head, giving him the look of some martyred saint, though in fact he was naturally bald. He hardly appeared fit for the combat of Vatican intrigues, for he was a gentle man.

Father Marcel folded the letter back into its envelope and questioned the wisdom of seeing Lee again. He expected he would find him much changed: it had been twelve years since their last meeting. Lee had been a young man then, and, the priest reflected, would always seem young to him. Father Marcel, at the time of their last meeting, had still been a virgin. Now, at age sixty, cheery, bemused, and fascinated, he had flowered in ways he had not dreamed possible; he had found much support from Lee, who encouraged him in his exploration of life's possibilities, and Father Marcel would always be grateful to him.

However, it did not seem likely that he would find time to visit Lee on this trip, a thought engendering a familiar spasm of guilt. Indeed, Father Marcel had a very special purpose on this visit, one that he anticipated with a thrill, a delicious shudder of potentiality. He had recently obtained membership in a club, an exclusive and discreet organization that arranged meetings between older gentlemen, like himself, and younger men who desired them. A man from Cincinnati had written to him, and he sounded charming: youthful, earnest, enthusiastic, ennobled with qualities to melt the already-soft heart of this globe-trotting monk-administrator. Certainly a visit to the chapter house in Tennessee was in order; diverting his journey there to include a stay in Cincinnati would not be difficult. He lost himself in a reverie on the mysteries of Cincinnati, the possible epiphany of the earnest and enthusiastic young man. Then the attendant stopped beside his seat and asked if he would like a drink.

Father Marcel looked up at the young woman and started: for a moment he saw his dead mother's face in this woman's. "Campari and soda," he said, steadying himself.

He suddenly realized that he hadn't thought of his mother for several weeks, and this troubled him. His mother had been a wonderful woman, he reminded himself, the most important person in his life. He began to reflect on his mother's great virtues, her patience and compassion, her complete devotion to him and to the Church. Then, quite without meaning to, he lost all thought of his mother and began to make a mental list of his boyfriends: Neville in London, Bruno in Munich, Tangathurai in New Delhi, Peter in San Francisco, Pablo and Juan in Madrid — which was worrisome; he didn't like juggling two romances, lying to one and then the other — and Felipe in Manila. And now, perhaps, the young man in Cincinnati. Having boyfriends was among the great discoveries of his life. He leaned his head back and jostled the ice cubes in his Campari and soda. Life was truly wonderful, he thought, in spite of the terrible reality of the world. His own life had been blessed with remarkable good fortune; he was happy to be alive.

✳

Six months after his visit to Cincinnati, Father Marcel adjusted the sheet of paper in his typewriter, then debated the wisdom of writing the letter he had in mind. He was back in Rome on this spring day, enjoying a few months of not traveling the globe. He sat beneath the filtered shade of a small lime tree, on a small folding chair, before an equally small table, which supported his portable Olivetti. The air was sweet, the sky nicely blue, the small courtyard — surrounded by its ochre-and-golden walls — pleasingly Mediterranean. He would be making another visit to New York soon. He had been invited by the archbishop of New York to assist with a mass at St. Patrick's, in honor of the order's 750th anniversary. He felt very strongly that he should reconnect with Lee on this visit.

His concern for this old friend of his American days had grown considerably; it saddened him to see Lee gradually becoming crazed with anger, to see him lose perspective because of his obsession with gay issues. Couldn't Lee remember that all human beings must struggle with the problems of being alive? Couldn't he see that the issue was not so much to protect gay men and women as to create a world permeated with Christ's teachings — a world of compassion and forgiveness, a world that accepted weakness of the flesh as the human condition, but that challenged abuse and exploitation of fellow humans, that condemned violence, aggression, and inhumanity? Father Marcel decided that, yes, he had to point out to Lee this fruitless waste of his energy. God knows it wasn't easy being a gay man in this world, but Lee must not let himself be blinded to his own participation in the family of man. Father Marcel believed he could be of much help to Lee on this matter. He finished typing his brief letter to Lee, added a handwritten postscript to say that they really must try to see each other, then sealed it in an envelope. He looked about him, taking pleasure in the cozy, bright setting and the Italian sky, which expansively filled his heart. It was good to be alive.

His desire to see Lee again was genuine, but Father Marcel had other, more compelling goals. On his previous trip to the United States, the young man in Cincinnati, who had sounded so simple and admirable, had proven to be a man of much complexity. He was indeed kind and admirable, but he was also very rough trade. The young man had asked Father Marcel to don certain leather-and-metal garments, if you could call them that, then to tie the young man's hands behind his back and "torture" him. At first the priest didn't understand, but with gentle coaxing from the young man, he began to learn what was expected of him. Father Marcel found himself intrigued and fascinated. He didn't know much about sadomasochism, but as he had never been a judgmental person, and knew only too well how weak people could be (himself included), he allowed himself to be open to this form of behavior. He did not enjoy "punishing" the young man, but he was mesmerized by the young man's intensity.

It was the young man (as observed by Father Marcel) who achieved another level of being, escaping from the here-and-now world and for a few minutes experiencing something beyond, something the priest guessed might be significant. As he continued to observe the young man, something happened: Father Marcel experienced a very clear understanding that he still had much to explore. A door — one he never knew existed — had quietly opened, gently beckoning, and beyond it lay a path of interesting possibilities. He watched the young man closely and shuddered. He felt his insides tighten. The inventory of his entire consciousness was being reorganized. His previous concepts of goodness and virtue had calmly been relocated, turned upside down, so to speak, and he perceived the intense, possibly purifying quality of total submission.

The priest understood that he could not dismiss this path abruptly; it required his attention. For several years now he had longed for abnegation of himself, for complete union with universal being. He had tried to find this via the Church; he sought complete humility; he submerged himself in Christ. He gave this effort up when he discovered his humility was false. It was but a fiction for pride, for the delight he took in being a paradox: poor but epicurean; humble but saucy, dapper, winning, irresistible; charming the worldliest of men and women, yet still a modest monk. Then he had chosen the way of self-discovery; he allowed himself to enjoy the world, the travel, the elegant dinners, and eventually the men. Perhaps this was what God had intended for him: to experience pleasure but to suffer from want of feeling real.

During this phase of worldly spirituality, he took shelter in a "childlike" faith, a willful acceptance of simplistic belief. He knew even at the time that it was not authentic.

He was an adult, not a child; his soul wasn't sufficiently simple to allow for childlike innocence. And yet, he believed, he never doubted his commitment to Christ and to living as nearly the Christian life as he was able. Which led him to seek out this new form of experience, an experience that would release him from who he was in the world. He had no interest whatever in partaking of S/M as an activity in itself. He saw it only as a possible path toward regaining himself. It might turn out not to be useful to him at all. He simply knew he was searching; he was on a quest.

Father Marcel closed up the typewriter, then took from a plain envelope a copy of *Drummer* given to him by the young man in Cincinnati. He read the articles — for perhaps the tenth time — with great interest, pondered the photographs with even greater interest, and studied the personal ads carefully. Some sounded intriguing. He decided, finally, to respond to a few of them, describing his purposes. (Rome, he wisely reasoned, was not the place to pursue this particular avenue of experience.) Then he noticed that one of the ads included a telephone number, which he knew to be in New Jersey. He looked at the clock; it might be around midnight in New Jersey. Still, he decided to place the call.

Father Marcel felt his heart pounding as he dialed the number. He felt he was placing a long-distance call to his destiny.

❋

In faraway New Jersey, a persistent phone, rudely ringing, woke Rick Rosenberg, drawing up from a deep and much-needed sleep the six feet and two hundred pounds of him. "Hello," he growled into the receiver.

"I hope I'm not calling too late," Father Marcel said.

"Whaddya want?" Rick was accustomed to getting phone calls at any hour of the day or night. It was to be expected when you put your number in an ad; he felt an obligation to take all calls seriously.

51

"You sound like quite a man."

Rick slipped into his master mode. "I *said*, what do you want?" Rick demanded.

"I need someone who understands what discipline is."

"You got him. What do you look like?"

Father Marcel paused, then decided there was no need to tell the truth at this point. "Tall, 190, eight inches."

"How big's your chest?"

Good grief, how should he know? What was a big chest? "Fifty inches."

"Fifty? Are you fat?"

"No."

"Fifty is very big."

"Forty-four."

"That's more like it." Rick had played this game many times. It was understood that he and the caller would fabricate their personal descriptions in this initial interview. He had learned to work through each one patiently, always alert for some interesting twist, some unusual taste, or some intriguing data. He knew he had to exercise caution when he listened to descriptions and dimensions; he yearned to believe all the men who claimed to have 30-inch waists, 20-inch biceps, 47-inch chests, and creamy bubbly butts, cleanly demarcated by tan lines. Muscles, he was a sucker for muscles. But experience had taught him that they couldn't be trusted, at least over the telephone.

"How about you? What do you look like?" Father Marcel asked.

"Five-eleven, 180, big tits, fat dick."

"Cut or uncut?"

"Cut."

"Jewish?" A Jew would be even better.

"Catholic."

"What's your name?"

"Bill," Rick said. "What's yours?"

"Father O'Malley."

"*Father* O'Malley? You a priest or something?"

"Yes, I am."

"Interesting. I haven't had any dealings with a priest for quite some time."

"Maybe it's time you did."

"What are you looking for?"

Another pause. Father Marcel could hardly tell this distant voice that he wanted to experience a total dissolution of this person he knew as "Father Marcel." He could not say he was looking for union with pure being as represented by the Incarnation of Christ in the world. "I'm looking for someone who can make me appreciate his power over me. I'm looking for someone who can teach me to let go of my pride."

Sounds promising, thought Rick. "Sounds a little vague to me," he said.

He's right, thought Father Marcel. "That's why I need discipline. I need definition."

"How old are you?" Rick asked.

"Forty-five."

Rick knew he was lying. Still, he would be interested in a priest; he wasn't sure why, he just knew he was.

"Well," said Rick, languorously, "I might be able to help a 45-year-old priest who needs definition."

"I bet you can." Father Marcel's breath became shorter. "What would you do?"

"I don't think I want to go into that right now."

Father Marcel experienced a tremor. He had not dreamed how tantalizing this could become. "When will you?"

"Later. Well, it was okay talking to you. Keep in touch."

"Wait—"

Rick hung up the phone, calculating that it would ring again in ninety seconds. After two minutes and forty seconds it rang; it was the priest again. "What do you want?" Rick pretended to be annoyed.

53

"I want to see you."

"I usually don't arrange meetings after just one telephone call. I like to get to know people first."

"Oh." Father Marcel hadn't counted on that. "I see. It's just that I'm going to be in New York in a couple of weeks."

"Where are you now?"

Father Marcel pondered his answer. "California."

"And you want to see me when you get here?"

"Yes, I'd like that very much."

"I don't know. I'll have to think about it. Why don't you leave me a number where I can call you?"

"I can't do that."

"Well, call me back in a few days."

Father Marcel yielded. "All right."

And so negotiations continued. Rick continued to put off the priest, who sounded like he would be truly boring as a playmate; yet he was attracted by the image of abusing a member of the Catholic clergy. It was necessary, therefore, to avoid seeing this Father O'Malley as a man and instead envision him only as the embodiment of Catholicism. Yes, he would like to have a whack at him.

Father Marcel, for a few days thereafter, became obsessed with the idea of meeting "Bill." The man clearly seemed knowledgeable in the ways of human relationships; he seemed skilled at making people suffer; he knew what he wanted; he drew very clear lines. Would it work? Could it?

"I have a confession," Father Marcel said in another phone call. "I don't look quite the way I said."

"What do you look like?"

"Well, not bad for someone my age. But not muscular. And not tall."

"Well, I guess I'll have to work with what you've got."

After several such phone conversations, during which Rick was explicit about what he would expect (including humiliation in the form of housework), and what the priest could expect from him, Rick finally agreed to allow "Father O'Malley" to visit him.

Rick awaited this meeting with little anticipation. It would be small potatoes, not a memorable encounter among his many extraordinary, sexually annihilating nights; this would be at most an interesting footnote. Father Marcel was not so indifferent. He approached the day with growing anxiety, with apprehension, with sweaty palms, with fear and dread. There was the possibility of realizing all he sought — the fearful prospect of pain, of ugliness, which he hoped could be transformed into beauty and insight — and of course, there was the possibility that this was simply another wrong path, and he would be not better off than he already was.

❋

On the second night of his New York trip, Father Marcel sat in the living room of the man he had arranged to meet. "Bill" confessed to being named Rick. No last name. The priest gazed at Rick with an instant of disbelief: the man was strikingly handsome, his physical reality more unsettling than the priest's fantasy. Rick's body was big, muscular, intimidating; his face was dark, his features chiseled and angular. In his dark brown eyes, Father Marcel could detect little warmth. Father Marcel began to feel a little uneasy; he decided to continue calling himself "Father O'Malley."

He found the room to be extremely unattractive: fake Biedermaier furniture, kitschy Meissen figurines, ugly green walls — how could anybody stand to live in such a place? He was growing impatient. Rick had picked him up at the Carlyle, then brought him to his house in the suburbs. Then he simply disappeared. He had brought Father Marcel in and told him to sit down and wait. "Where will you be?" Father Marcel had asked.

Rick had given him a menacing look. "I said *wait*. And don't ask questions. I'll get you when I'm ready."

It seemed like a long time. Rick looked Jewish, which pleased the priest. In this endeavor he hoped to approximate, symbolically if not actually, the suffering that Christ had known. It would be that much more real if it were at the hands of a Jew. His purpose, as he knew, was not so much to suffer physical pain as to shed himself of this personage he had grown so weary of: the affable charmer, the good son, the man who had lost his Christian simplicity and his connection with Christ. That hardly seemed likely in the present circumstances. This adventure gave every sign of becoming artificial, a pseudo experience; he now doubted it would prove meaningful, and it certainly would not achieve for him mystical union with Christ. What on the surface might appear awful and degrading would in reality turn out simply to be trite and juvenile. What might appear to stretch one's comprehension of existence could well turn out to be dull and empty. He hoped it wouldn't be like that. Desire for another meaningless experience was not what brought him here.

Suddenly the lights went out throughout the house. Had there been a power failure? He peered through the window. No, the other houses still had light. He sat up straight, made himself very still, placed his knees together, and folded his hands in his lap. He could feel that something was about to happen. He waited; silence. Then footsteps on the stairs. Father Marcel quietly drew in a deep breath. Still very quietly, no more footsteps; then he heard Rick breathing softly. At least he assumed it was Rick. Father Marcel waited, tense, his heart pounding; why wasn't the man doing something?

Finally, after what seemed a long silence, Rick spoke. "Come with me," he said. Father Marcel said nothing, and remained motionless.

"I said, come with me." His voice sounded threatening. "What do you say?"

"Yes, sir?"

"That's right. And don't forget it."

"No, sir."

"This way."

Father Marcel followed him in the darkness, clinging to the stair rail as they descended into Rick's basement. They entered a room. "Over here," Rick ordered. Father Marcel searched the black space with outstretched hands. "Here," Rick said. "Stand right here." Father Marcel stopped moving. "Take off your clothes." Father Marcel removed his shoes and socks, his jacket and pants, his underpants, his shirt, his collar. He heard the serpentine clinking of metal moving against itself: a chain. Then the cold steel against his neck; he reared back instinctively. "It's okay," Rick said, soothing him. "It's a heavy chain collar and a padlock. I want you to wear it to please me. All right?"

Father Marcel released a breath. "Yes, sir."

"Is this your first time?"

"Yes, sir."

"Any questions?"

"I guess I'm not sure about the pain." Father Marcel wished he could see Rick. The darkness was disturbing. The touch of Rick's hand on his skin was not reassuring.

"This isn't about pain," Rick said. "It's about trust. It's about limits. It's about reaching the fine line that separates fear from experience. You have to bring yourself up to the line, and then you have to cross it. Do you follow me?"

"Yes, sir."

"Pain is purely a mental experience. What for some people may be pain is for others pleasure. But trust is real. You will learn to trust me. And you will eventually discover that I have to trust you as well. I will subject you to certain experiences that may be new to you. They may feel uncomfortable at first. If you feel you are not ready to continue, at any point, you will signal that to me with a code word."

"What's the word? Sir."

"The word is *freedom*."

"Freedom?"

"You don't like it? Then pick another word."

"No, it's fine."

"Remember that I am your master now."

He heard Rick walk away from him, and then the sound of a light switch being flicked. A narrow beam of blue light shot down from above, directly over Rick's head. He stood with his feet planted apart, his head lowered. Father Marcel couldn't see his eyes, only shadows beneath the brim of his leather cap. He wore black leather boots. A harness of leather straps circled his waist, crossed his shoulders, strained against his broad, hairy chest, encircled his genitals, leaving his dick and balls free. On his wrists were leather cuffs studded with steel. In one hand he held a short riding crop, which he slapped against his other hand.

"Come over here," Rick said slowly.

Father Marcel didn't move. He stared at this figure before him, transfixed by the beauty of Rick's body, by his presence, and annoyed by the phoniness of his getup and the pose he had struck. Far from losing himself, Father Marcel felt acutely conscious of being a person in a particular place at a particular time, conscious of the beautiful body before him that had been trashed up in leather and stultifying attitudes, and exceedingly conscious that this would be a slightly ludicrous exercise, a so-called attempt to go to "the limits." How we delude ourselves, the priest reflected. Well, he had gotten himself into this mess; he would follow through with it. He knew this would require considerable tact on both their parts.

"I said, come over here." Father Marcel took a step toward Rick. "*Crawl.* Get down on your knees. And don't look up at me."

Father Marcel crawled across the cold bare concrete floor. He stopped when he could see the toe of Rick's boot just before his eyes. "Lick my boot," Rick said. This was so ridiculous, thought the monk; however, etiquette demanded that he comply. Father Marcel placed his tongue on Rick's boot, jolted by a terrible taste — what was it? Shoe polish? Alum? Urine? He moved from the toe to the ankle, then toward the rim of the boot. His cheek brushed against the hair of Rick's leg.

Suddenly, seized by a jolt of unexpected desire, he wanted him; he craved every tiny hair, every surface, every contour, the body, the man. No, he said to himself, this is merely a charade, I am merely playing a role. Yet his cynicism failed him; a profound need engulfed him as he drowned in desire. His tongue, driven by growing lust, slid onto the skin of Rick's leg.

"Not yet!" Rick said. His voice was low, mean, seductive. Father Marcel could not longer restrain himself; he pressed his mouth against Rick's leg. Then he felt the quick searing lash of Rick's whip slicing the air, a piercing snap of brittle sound, followed by a stinging sensation across his buttocks. His heart sank; he trembled. This man was evil, the devil come to test his soul.

"Now the other boot," Rick ordered.

Father Marcel began to lick the other boot. He felt himself sinking, losing sense of where he was. Then a sudden panic: he felt very close to letting go. Could he do it? Could he surrender himself to this evil master? Could he give up being himself? Rick was making sounds: words, perhaps, pushing him on, permitting him, ordering him to touch his skin, his flesh. Father Marcel was lost in the intense reality of the moment. He would go with this man anywhere.

"Now I think we're ready to get down to business," Rick said.

❋

Rick woke the next morning, stretched his arms above his head, lay back, and stared at the ceiling. He heard Trixie, his peek-a-poo, padding across the floor and called her to him. She hopped into bed with him and licked his nose.

"Good little doggie," he murmured. He looked at the clock, which showed quarter of twelve.

He remembered the old man downstairs and groaned. He would have to untie him. What a bummer last night had been. He had never been into old men, nor had he ever cared for the pure exercise of degradation and humiliation. It only meant something to him when done with the right slave. He had thought — wrongly — that having a priest for a slave would be a turn-on. It wasn't. A hunky young priest, maybe, but not this one. So it had been a big bore. Well, at least he had made him scrub the bathroom; that was useful.

He got up, put on jeans and a t-shirt, and went down to his basement. There he greeted Father Marcel with a smile. "You doing all right?" Father Marcel, exhausted, his eyes hollow and forlorn, nodded. "Just very sleepy," he said.

"Well, you can get a nap soon." Rick undid the manacles that secured the priest to the wall, removed the clips from his nipples and the clothespins from his penis, then released the chains around his ankles. Father Marcel began to massage his wrists. "It doesn't hurt, does it?" Rick asked. Father Marcel shook his head. "You're very quiet. Is something wrong?"

"No, nothing's wrong. I'm still just sorting through all this."

Rick was concerned. The old man said he was okay, but he didn't look okay. Rick doubted that his guest could be in pain; he had barely touched him all night, just nipped him with the crop and slapped him a bit. He was probably just stiff from the chains. "I hope it was what you wanted."

"It was, it was." Father Marcel took a step and stumbled. Rick caught him and held him upright.

"Tell me where it hurts," Rick said.

Father Marcel looked at him; there was no answer to this question. The pain could not be located in his body. He looked into Rick's eyes, and saw there not the personification of evil, nor the Antichrist, nor a misguided soul; he saw, or experienced, the presence of another human being sharing in the process of being alive. He began to cry. Rick pulled him close and wrapped his arms around him. Father Marcel then wept copiously.

"It's okay," Rick said. He was gentle with Father Marcel, very caring. "You went somewhere you didn't know about, and it scared you, but now you're back. And you got something good out of this. You learned to trust me. Right?"

"Right."

"Good. Well, come on, get your clothes on. I'll fix some breakfast."

"That's very kind of you."

"I always fix breakfast for company."

While Rick cooked the eggs and bacon, Father Marcel got dressed, then sat down gently, mindful of his tender bottom. Rick told Father Marcel about his life, about his lover's death from AIDS, about his rage at the government, about living in the midst of a plague. Father Marcel was not really interested. His mind was somewhere else.

When Father Marcel got back to the Carlyle, he slept for six hours.

※

The next day, a warm afternoon, Father Marcel went to Central Park to work on the piece he would deliver at St. Patrick's Cathedral. He sat on a bench under the tall shading oaks of the mall with a small notebook and pen and wrote down his principal points. First was the founding and history of the order, then its current goals and accomplishments, then the relevance of this work to New York Catholics, and, lastly, some words of reassurance and support in this troubled world. It would be a simple presentation; he was not out to make an impression. He wrote for a few minutes, enjoying the soft warm breeze, undisturbed by the masses of people around him, by the blaring radios, the skaters, bikers, or by sirens screaming in the distance.

He finished writing, closed his notebook, and began to reflect on the events of the preceding evening with Rick. It had been a mistake, a big, stupid mistake. He could argue that meeting someone like Rick was certainly worthwhile, an education in itself. And perhaps his wish to lose himself in what he imagined to be "pure being" had some merit; through personal effacement, through humiliation, he might have freed himself from the prison of his existence. But that didn't happen. Father Marcel knew his approach had been faulty. He sought what could not be found. He smiled ruefully, remembering the famous question *Why seek ye the living among the dead?* True, he had experienced a kind of loss of self; indeed, it was rather considerable. Thinking about it now, he could say that he ceased to be himself and became part of a comprehensive void unrestricted by time and space.

That, he felt, was where the mistake lay. What useful purpose could there possibly be in finding oneself in a void? Who wanted to be part of a void? Even if you wanted to call it "pure being," a void still amounted to nothing. Worse still, it seemed that in such a state, where you became "nothing," you also needed nothing. He had wanted to participate with Christ in the necessary act of losing himself, of losing his romance with life — yet if he could do this for himself, would he then need the intercession of Christ? No. And if not, what was the Christian religion all about? He felt now that he had been seriously misguided in his attempt. If his evening with Rick had provided any glimpse of eternity, Father Marcel sincerely hoped eternity did not exist. No, it couldn't have been that; Christ still remained for him. Father Marcel experienced a pronounced relief at knowing he did not have to be the agent of his own salvation. He sincerely, silently thanked Rick for

62

allowing him to renew the presence of Christ in his life. It had been a narrow escape.

He walked back to the Carlyle, to all onlookers a trim, dapper sixty-year-old man, full of himself. He had to get ready for an evening with the archbishop. What a strange few days these had been. I am a simple man, he thought; I will simply have to live my life as best I can.

Jameson Currier   Reunions

"Imagine," Glenn said. "The idea of it."

We were seated at a window table that looked out onto Eighth Avenue. A bright crack of sunlight bent through the glass and landed on a row of bottles behind the tall, dark mahogany bar. It was late morning and the restaurant was empty. Glenn was on his second martini; I was still sipping my first beer. Though I have known Glenn for almost a decade, we hadn't seen each other in almost three months. Our communication had been limited to phone conversations and notes left in our friend Peter's apartment. After Peter's funeral service, an hour earlier, we had walked the three blocks to this restaurant.

Glenn had just finished telling me the story of when Peter, in the hospital, decided he hated his nurse, a Turkish woman, so much that one day he started insulting her in French, which she didn't understand. The nurse thought because Peter kept saying "chienne," "chienne," he meant he wanted the channel changed on the television set beside the bed. I looked down at the table feeling momentarily guilty of my smile, then fingered my necktie, blue silk with tiny white dots.

I was surprised to see Glenn looking calm and rested. I felt both miserable and uneasy, having helped Peter's family with the details for the funeral. Glenn looked terrific, perhaps the best I had ever seen him: he had cut his light brown hair short on the sides and in the back, his complexion was clear and healthy, red at the cheeks, and in his dark, tailored suit and striped tie he looked like a schoolboy who had just cut class.

"And you know about the last time he saw Kyle, don't you?" Glenn said, his brown eyes widening.

"I didn't know they saw each other," I answered. "I thought they just spoke on the phone."

"When they were both in the mood."

"When did he see him?"

"Just a couple of weeks ago."

"He probably forgot to tell me about it."

"He didn't forget about it. He was too busy being cranky. 'I need the tissues by the bed,'" he said, mimicking the way Peter would demand things. "'You know this soup is too hot for me. But I don't want to watch *Casablanca* on TV.'"

I laughed again. In the last few months, when Peter wasn't in the hospital, Glenn had stayed at Peter's apartment during the mornings and afternoons, helping with the cleaning, cooking, shopping, and laundry; I had helped out at night after work. Both of us had tried to keep Peter comfortable. He had dropped a lot of weight, the medications made him drowsy and incoherent at times, and he had lost a great deal of mobility because of the pains in his legs, the cause of which a squad of doctors and specialists couldn't discover or control. And every day we tried to keep him entertained, never an easy feat even when he was well. Many times we were both driven close to tears by Peter's bitterness over being sick, the constant stress of trying to relieve his anxieties, and our own helplessness and confusion, watching our friend grow weaker and weaker every day. Suddenly, I felt an odd tranquility: part sadness, part reprieve, part lightness from drinking beer on an empty stomach so early in the day.

"His nurse, the one that came to his apartment, told me it was because of the steroids," I said. "She said if he was cranky before he started them, they would only make it worse."

A waiter approached the table, and we ordered another round of drinks. "Why is it that all the beauty in New York seems to be wasted on the waiters?" Glenn said as we watched our waiter, muscular and quite handsome with a dark mustache as wide as a comb, rock his hips as though dancing as he glided behind the bar.

"He wasn't just cranky before," Glenn said to me, though his attention was still focused on the waiter. "He was always particular. I mean, remember the time he canceled his subscription to the opera because they started to flash subtitles above the stage?"

The waiter returned to the table and placed the drinks on top of fresh napkins, scooping the empty glasses and bottle up with one hand. Glenn looked up and smiled. The waiter caught his eye and grinned, somewhat embarrassed, and asked, "Anything else?"

"Just a lot of wishes," Glenn said, lifting his martini glass in the air and shaking it lightly. The waiter made an uncomfortable bow and departed again toward the bar.

"Anyway, Kyle had been sick for a long time, almost two years," Glenn said, and replaced his drink on top of the napkin. "At that point he was worse off than Peter. He had just gotten out of the hospital a few days earlier. And he was just like Peter: the type that couldn't sit still. Well, it must have been like ten o'clock in the morning, and Peter was already in a bad mood because he hadn't been able to keep any of his breakfast down. I was washing the dishes when Kyle called and said he was coming over. You should have seen the look of surprise on Peter's face. He made me stop what I was doing and find him a clean shirt and clean underwear, pick up the sheets from the floor, make the bed, and put new batteries in the electric razor. The whole time he kept mumbling, 'He's never going to make it up the stairs.' About an hour later the buzzer rings, and I tell Peter I'll go down and help Kyle up the stairs. Well, Peter started going wild and said that if Kyle had enough energy to walk around the block from his apartment, he could certainly make it up five flights of stairs without any help, and it would only make him mad if someone offered to help him. I mean, I could tell Peter was a little angry because he hadn't had the energy to go out of the apartment in almost a week. So we both sat on the sofa and waited. And waited. About thirty minutes later there was this soft knock on the door."

"How did Kyle look?"

"He was real thin," Glenn replied. "He had always been a little on the chubby side, but his arms had gotten so skinny he looked like one of those people I used to make with my dad's pipe cleaners when I was a kid. He looked worse than Peter ever did. He lost most of his hair, but he had grown a beard. It made his face look so dark and glum.

"Anyway, he was standing in the doorway wobbling back and forth, and the first words out of his mouth are, 'I think I'm going to faint.' But he makes it over to the chair near the television by himself, and he sits down. Peter wouldn't get up, because he didn't want Kyle to know he had to use a cane to walk. So they sat and talked a while: Kyle said his roommate had set up a computer for him on a rolling tray so that he could play video games in bed, and Peter started remembering about the time they missed the bus coming back from Atlantic City because they couldn't pull Kyle away from the nickel slot machines. Then they both started complaining about their doctors and medicines. And then Kyle gets up and turns on the TV. Well, of course Kyle turned the channel to MTV, which I could tell made Peter livid, because, you know him, if it wasn't pre-1960 or British it wasn't worth watching. But they sat there and talked some more.

"They seemed fine, so I told them I was going out to run some errands," Glenn continued. "I had to get Peter's new prescription filled at the pharmacy, and I thought they might like some time alone. I must have been gone for about an hour and when I got back, they were both gone. No note. Nothing. I sort of panicked — I mean, these were not two young men in prime-time health. I even looked out the window just to make sure they hadn't jumped. I never thought they could have made it down the stairs and out of sight before I got back."

"How did Peter make it down the stairs?"

"He told me he had to help Kyle down."

"What?"

"They were sort of balancing each other. And Peter didn't even take his cane. When one wobbled, the other one sort of wobbled the other way."

"I can't believe it."

"Anyway, I thought about calling someone, but who do I call? 'Hello, police, I'd like to report two missing homosexuals.' Then I thought maybe one of them had collapsed. If Kyle had needed help, Peter would have called an ambulance. If it were Peter, he would probably still have been on the floor. I didn't think it possible both of them would need to go to the hospital. So I went across the hall and asked that Hispanic lady if she had seen them. If anything had happened, she would have been the first to know. But she hadn't seen them. So I went back inside and called Kyle's number, thinking maybe they had gone there, but there wasn't any answer."

"What did you do?"

"I just waited. About two hours later the buzzer rang, and when I listened, it was Peter yelling for some money."

"Money?"

"The two of them had gone for a cab ride, but neither of them had any money."

"Where did they go?"

"To the park. They drove around Central Park for two hours!"

"But Peter hated Central Park."

"Well, by the time I got downstairs with some money Peter was fuming. He had dropped Kyle off at his apartment. He had one of those cab drivers who doesn't speak English, and he kept telling the cab driver to go up the stairs and buzz the apartment so he could get paid. Anyway, Peter got so frustrated he opened the door of the cab and literally crawled up the steps to ring the buzzer. And the whole time this cab driver, who must have been just off the boat from South America, was flapping his arms and screaming, 'Pay me trip. Pay me trip.'"

"How much did the cab cost?"

"Over fifty dollars. Peter didn't want to tip the driver because he was a 'first-class idiot.' I calmed the cab driver down, paid him, and helped Peter up the stairs. He complained the whole time. He said that after I left to go shopping, Kyle decided he was hungry, so he went into the kitchen and found the chocolate chip ice cream in the freezer and sat down in front of the TV and ate the whole pint. And he was still hungry. So they decided to go down to the store on the corner to get some more. By the time they got to the bottom of the stairs, Kyle was huffing and puffing so much that they couldn't go anywhere, not even back up the stairs. They flagged down a cab, but the driver wouldn't take them half a block. So Kyle decided they should drive through Central Park."

Glenn pushed aside his empty glass. "On top of it all, the driver had no idea where anything in the city was.

When Kyle said 'Central Park,' he must have thought he meant 'Centre Street,' because they started heading downtown. When Peter realized they were heading in the wrong direction, he started tapping the driver on the shoulder and saying 'No, No,' which got the driver real annoyed. He finally got the driver to turn around, but by the time they got to the park, Kyle had fallen asleep."

"What?"

"He kept falling asleep. They drove all through the park, and Peter kept nudging Kyle, because he was sleeping with his head on Peter's shoulder and hurting his arm. Kyle would wake up for a minute and then pass out again. When Peter told the driver to take them back, he got lost again. They ended up on the West Side Highway. So two hours later the cab pulled up in front of Kyle's apartment, and Peter woke him up and helped him to the door and then told the driver to take him around the corner to his apartment. But you want to know what made Peter really furious?" Glenn asked.

"What?"

"That Kyle had eaten all of his ice cream. The reason he had agreed so hastily to go to the store with Kyle was because he was afraid Kyle would eat the butterscotch cake Suzanne made for him. Imagine, two *faygelahs* riding through Central Park, one mad because the other had eaten all of his ice cream, the other so oblivious to everything he simply falls asleep, with a driver who doesn't even know what the hell he's doing. Two hours later I'm sure they forgot they had even seen each other."

✳

A week after Peter saw Kyle, Kyle died. Peter died less than a month later. Six months later I sat in a restaurant telling my friend Larry this story. We had both been drinking steadily for over an hour since we'd finished eating, and as we were leaving I waited with him at the corner to make sure he caught a cab. Watching him drive away, I was again baffled by the absurd uncertainty that had crept into my life. Glenn had gone quickly; overnight a cold had turned into pneumonia. Two days later he was dead. The last time I had seen him was the day of Peter's funeral, when he told me the story about the cab ride through Central Park. Walking uptown to my apartment I remembered the way Peter would turn to me after we had walked out of a movie or a play or a restaurant and shove his hands deeply into his pants pockets and shrug his shoulders, knowing he was not yet ready to go home, and say, "Whatever should we do next?"

Randy Boyd Hostage

The impact of LeRon's forearm crashing against the bedroom door was so violent he could feel the blood immediately gush through his arm, almost causing him to drop the gun. A ringing nausea stung the insides of his head, temporarily blinding him. He stumbled through the door. As soon as he regained his balance, he pointed the gun all around the room he had spent the first eighteen years of his life in. The lights were out, the windows covered with blankets. He squinted, trying to figure out what to blow away first as he began screaming:

"Get up! Get your shiftless black asses out of bed!"

Both his brothers were lying there as he knew they would be, sleeping in the middle of the day like two lazy bums, as they'd done for twenty-six and thirty-one fucking years. That's all the fuck they did. Sleep, then terrorize, then sleep some more. To think *they* were older and supposed to set the example for *him*.

"Get up!" he shouted. "Somebody's gonna pay."

"What—" James yelled, all gruff and half-asleep.

"Muthafucka—" Darrin said, jolting wake with the kind of panic he was probably used to, since he was a fucking two-bit dope dealer.

"LeRon?" James rubbed his eyes quickly.

"That's right, the pussy," LeRon said. "Now wake the fuck up!"

It had been a month since he had been in the house visiting Moma and a year since he had been in this damn bedroom, this dark, dingy hellhole he'd shared with James and Darrin as a kid. It still smelled like a fucking locker room — stinking clothes thrown everywhere, the fucking pictures on the wall lopsided, broken sports trophies, pussy magazines, dirty dishes, drug paraphernalia. Thank God — or who the fuck ever — he'd gotten out of here — and South Central L.A. — when he did, else he'd be sleeping here in the middle of the fucking day and selling dope at night just like his two bum-assed brothers.

"Get the fuck up—"

He wanted to fire the gun right then to show them he was for real, but James saw the shiny black barrel and jumped up in his filthy bed, sitting on the edge and grabbing onto the mattress.

"Get some fucking light in here." LeRon rushed over and yanked at the stale-smelling blanket that covered the window. "Middle of the goddamned day and you two are fucking sleeping your life away."

The blanket came off, sunlight flooded the room, dust floated everywhere around them. Out the window, he saw the concrete floor of the backyard, then the little shed where James and Darrin used to bring girls.

"What the fuck are you doing, man?" Darrin sat up.

"I came here — I don't know why I came here — all I know is somebody's gotta fucking pay. I've had enough."

"What you talking 'bout, boy?" James said in his threatening I'm-the-oldest voice. Both LeRon's brothers were

73

much bigger than him, but the gun was all the size he needed.

"Had enough what?" Darrin asked.

Were they taking him seriously? They'd better take him seriously. LeRon Davis wasn't going to be the pussy of the family anymore. Fuck life as he knew it, he'd thought on the way over here. Fuck the apartment in Culver City, fuck the job at the video store, fuck junior college. Fuck twenty-four years of shit, fuck feeling okay about being gay, fuck rappers and rap music. Fuck dying. Especially fuck dying.

"I'm sick of all this shit, sick of people like you two and—" LeRon glared at the framed poster of Big Daddy Kane — James's favorite rapper — on the wall, "—and him."

"He's gone off, man," Darrin whispered harshly to James.

"I ain't done shit." LeRon pointed the gun at Darrin, looking at him down the shaking barrel.

"Put that gun down, boy." James's voice rumbled as it had when they were kids and James was going to beat the shit out of him again.

"What do you want, man?" Darrin asked.

"Here, boy, give me the gun." James stood up.

"Don't look at me like I'm crazy." LeRon held the gun up higher, high enough to reach James's six-foot-four head. "I'm not the one who's crazy. I'm getting my college degree, I got a place on the west side. It may not be shit, but I got out of here. I got a job. Video Plus Video Store. We sell movies. I'm the fucking day manager. They trust me — stay back."

"Give me the gun, boy." James kept getting closer with that big-brother forcefulness.

"I said stay back."

That big-brother forcefulness he hated so much—

"Give me the gun."

Hated with a fucking motherfuck passion—

"Give ... me ... the gun."

"I said — stay ba—" He extended his arm and swung toward the poster of Big Daddy Kane. Fucking Big Daddy Kane. Fucking motherfucking rapper. He closed his eyes. The last thing he saw was James's arm reaching out—

POW!

The force of the gun threw LeRon against the wall behind him. His eyes popped open. Big Daddy Kane shattered in his own glass; the plaster on the wall erupted in skid marks. The room shook up and down like an earthquake, trophies falling, papers flying, the walls vibrating. James flew back onto the bed, his arms flailing, his legs buckling.

But there was no blood, only James's eyes, whiter and wider and more terrified than LeRon thought his oldest brother capable of. Everyone was still alive. For now.

No one outside would care about the shot, if they heard it at all.

"Get the fuck back," came from LeRon's insides, overruling the shock.

"Do what he says, man," Darrin told James.

"Damn straight," LeRon said with newfound conviction, looking at the scars on the wall, then his two brothers — bigger, stronger, more everything than him. Their tall, wide bodies had always towered over his short, thin frame. But now, now he was looking down on them, gun in hand — just a pistol, but it felt like a rapid-fire, military bazooka.

But the chaos in his head had to stop. He had to get his bearings. A few deep breaths.

A moment to think. He needed a moment to think.

Sweat dripped off his forehead, stinging his eyes like acid. He stood there frozen, unable to move or react or think, frozen like the time when he was a kid and James had caught him jacking off to that picture of O.J. Simpson.

Just one moment to think.

The last few hours had been so fast and furious ... he didn't know ... what to know ... get a grip ... quit shaking. The last few hours ... remember the last few hours ... a normal workday at the store ... leaving early ... the doctor's office ... almost passing out ... T-cells, immune suppressor cell ratio ... the freeway ... fucking rappers ... busting in the house ... Moma wasn't home ... no Dad ... he up and left when LeRon was a baby ... but his gun ... Dad's gun was still there ... loaded and hidden in a toolbox in the shed, his brothers' not-so-secret emergency weapon. Even Moma knew about it ... poor Moma.

Wait, that's it: things were getting clearer now. After the doctor's office, he drove here from Culver City, went to the garage, got the gun, and he wanted — justice?

His brothers were looking at him now like he was off — the same look he saw in their eyes as a child.

"I came here to get justice." His voice — the voice they always said was so soft and wispy — felt hoarse, but loud and strong.

He looked at the dead poster of Big Daddy Kane. Big Fucking Macho Real Man Daddy Kane. Then, then he glared at his brothers. Big Fucking Macho Real Men James and Darrin.

"You bastards have never understood me!" he yelled. "You never let me be. Just 'cause I was a fag. A fag! A fag! A fag!" he shouted, savoring the taste of the word, the first time he ever felt free to say that word so forcefully. "You made me that fucking faggot, always calling me a sissy—"

"Aw, man, I don't want to get into this shit," Darrin said.

"You never want to get into this shit, not when I was a kid and you just assumed I was a sissy, and not now when you know for sure. You never want to talk about it. You barely talk to me when I come to visit Moma, acting like you can't be around me more than two minutes. You never want to hear about my friends or my dates, not even what the fucking virus is doing to my body. Well, now we're gonna get into this shit and get into it good."

"We didn't make you no fag, man," Darrin said.

James broke in. "We said it's okay that you're gay. Didn't I tell you I love you anyway?"

"Last fucking year, last fucking year when I came out to the family. What else could you do when your little faggot brother says, 'I'm gay and, by the way, I just tested positive.' What about all the rest of my life? What about the first twenty-three years? Twenty-three years of hell, of feeling like a freak, just 'cause I didn't do the same things as you two when we were kids, just 'cause I sucked at sports, 'cause I didn't want to fight and play rough."

"What do you want from us, man?" Darrin asked. "Why'd you get the gun?"

"I don't know. I don't know. You held me back. You wouldn't let me be. Back then I wanted to be different. I saw you fucking up with your lives. You fucked up school; you fucked up basketball — too doped up to stay on *junior college* teams. You fucked up Moma — she had to work two jobs to feed your big asses. You fucked up women, beating 'em and treating 'em like shit. How many times have you made Tanita get an abortion, Darrin? How many girls have you knocked up, James? Would you even know?"

"Aw, man, fuck all that," Darrin said.

"Part of me said I was *not* going to be like that. I stayed away from the drugs, tried to be a good student, but you two were still better than me. You had the friends, the sports, the easygoing personalities. The only thing I had was a ball of confusion."

James started to speak, but LeRon stopped him by pointing the gun at him.

"Yeah," LeRon kept going, "I may have thought about being with guys when I was an adolescent, but I wanted to date the prettiest girls in school just like you two. I wanted to fit in and be good at sports. I wanted to be cool. But I couldn't. I was different. I didn't know the first thing about girls. I was too quiet to be liked. And you two had to terrorize me about it every day for the first eighteen years of my life.

"I was so fucking confused," he went on. "I wasn't cool. And I also wanted guys, but that was bad. That made me a fag. What the fuck was I supposed to do? It was like a war around here, you beating me up, taking my things, calling me a pussy. I didn't know what to do or how to feel or what to like. I couldn't even be with anybody for eighteen years. Till I moved away from here and this life."

"So you got your shit together now," James said.

"I got a shit *life* now, still trying to feel good about myself, fighting a fucking disease. And every guy I fall in love with is just like you — a straight, tough-acting fool who's too scared to let a sissyboy into his life. My friends tell me I go after these guys 'cause I was taught gay guys are weak and worthless and that I probably got that idea from my family. I can't even think straight about being gay now, thanks to you. My whole life you've held me hostage."

"Hostage?" Darrin said.

"Not free to be what I want, to feel whatever I'm feeling."

"Hostage!" Darrin repeated, like it was the most absurd thing he'd ever heard.

"*That's* what I'm doing," LeRon said as the idea struck home. "You held me hostage, now I'm holding you hostage. How does it feel, big brothers? Feel like a punk? You're letting a sissy control you. You're letting a pussy hold you hostage."

"Moma's gonna be back any minute—" James tried.

"Don't give me that shit. I know she's working both shifts at the beauty shop. She's the only one in this family I can relate to — the female." He let out a snide laugh.

78

"What are you complaining about?" Darrin said. "You got your job, your crib, your gay friends. Nobody stopped you."

"Everything I got now I kicked, clawed, and scratched for, 'cause I knew there had to be a better way than taking your shit for the rest of my life."

"What shit?" both his brothers said.

"What shit? Always putting me down as a kid. You, Darrin, calling me 'Swishman' 'cause of the way I walked. What the fuck was that for, huh? I'm supposed to be your fucking brother. Especially you, Darrin. We're almost the same age. Like the time we were over at Manny Blake's house — Moma made you take me with you. We're all sitting in his bedroom. I was twelve, and you and Manny were fourteen. I dribbled his basketball and he called me a faggot. *He called me a faggot.* And you just let it go, you just sat there and let him do it."

"I didn't either," Darrin began. "I remember that. I told him, 'Don't call him a faggot, man.'"

Darrin was right, wasn't he? The bastard.

"You barely told him," LeRon said. "In a soft voice under your breath. Like you were scared to stand up for me. And when I used to have to go with you to the park. You and your friends used to be out there playing ball, and I was on the sidelines pretending to be a gymnast on the balance beam at the Olympics. You let 'em make fun of me. I got hassled about wanting to be another Nadia Comaneci for years."

"What was I supposed to do?" Darrin asked.

"Take up for me, goddamnit. I'm your little brother. Tell me it's okay, that I can be whatever I wanna be, and I don't have to worry about what those guys think. But, no, *you* called me a punk."

"Why you bringing up shit that happened in the past?" James asked.

"And you." LeRon turned to James. "I fucking had a crush on you. You were seven years older. The hotshot teenager. I wanted your friends, your girls, your athletic ability, your sense of humor, your body."

"That's sick, man," Darrin said.

"You got your own shit," James said. "You had the book smarts. Moma always favored you—"

"Buuullshit," LeRon said. "She says she still loves me, but I know she'd rather have ten real men like you than one Moma's boy. Besides, we're not talking about Moma. I'm talking about my two big brothers, the two most important men in my life."

"All that shit's in the past, man," James said. "We been doing fine. Everybody knows you're gay now, and it ain't no big deal. We done told you we still love you—"

"Darrin's never said it."

"Bullshit," Darrin shouted. "I told you last year after you told us you had the AIDS virus. You came over one night after your group therapy and told me you felt good about your life, that you was still healthy and happy being gay, and you wanted to be close to the family, and you loved me. I told you I loved you too, right then, man. So why don't you put down that gun? That shit's in the past—"

"Past, my ass. If you hadn't made me a fag, I wouldn't be worried about dying right now—"

"You been dealing with it good. You all right and living and shit," Darrin said.

"You been doing all you can do," James added. They were trying to gang up on him, that's all they were trying to do.

"Well, maybe doing all I can do is not enough anymore. Maybe the one hundred and forty-six T-cells left in me are just too damn tired of fighting, fighting all the fucking infections that are everywhere, fighting all the prejudice and ignorance, fighting people like you."

"Something new happened," James said. "What happened?"

"I'm fucking tired."

"What is it, man?" Darrin insisted.

"I said I'm fucking tired."

"What happened?" Darrin pleaded with a quivering voice. LeRon didn't give one damn if those might be tears welling up in Darrin's eyes as he repeated, "What happened?"

"It's called life." LeRon sat down on the third bed, his old bed. "I've been sweating like a pig for six straight weeks. I've thrown up every other meal for the last week. Stuff's happening to my body. I just came from the doctor. Some kind of infection I can't even pronounce. Maybe the last one."

"We tell you we love you, man, and we care," James said.

"Now. Now when it's too late. Now when I could be dead in months, weeks — where were you then?"

"Man, we was all young then." Darrin's bullshit wisdom. "We didn't know shit."

"I know that," LeRon said. "I learn all about that shit every Wednesday night in my gay *awareness* group. Don't call it therapy, fucker. We're not crazy; we're just trying to get over all the shit the world and our families put us through. We learn that you didn't know any better, that you were just a product of a homophobic world. And yeah, I've felt better about being gay for the last few years, now that I got my own life and my *girl*friends. But I still got anger inside, and it won't go away. I'm not getting any better, and I'm fucking sick of thinking about dying before I know what it's like to be old, to find love, to have a career, to retire and travel, to see *thirty*, for God's sake. I might end up withering away to nothing, maybe weighing eighty pounds. You always got on me about being so small and wimpy at five-eight, a hundred and forty. What will you say when you visit me in the hospital and I'm eighty lifeless pounds? *If* you visit me—"

"Don't talk like that, man," Darrin said.

"Nothing. Nothing is worth that — not the hell you put me through for being gay, for sure. I'd rather be straight in a fucked marriage. I'd rather be as pathetic as you two are right now. Nothing is worth dying like I'm gonna die, and you did it to me." Suddenly LeRon's voice trailed off, and the room was still.

"I don't want to be eighty pounds," he said, almost whispering.

The three of them said nothing, their eyes shifting around the room, staring at a shot-up Big Daddy Kane, at the floor, at the broken sports trophies, at the gun, at each other but not for too long. Minutes passed, many many minutes.

LeRon still held the gun up high, chilling visions of Tehran and Beirut and brown men with wiry black beards and scary rifles running through his head. Must be easier for those men; they didn't care — they didn't know their hostages. Did they feel compassion for their prisoners? Why should he? Did Darrin and James ever feel compassion for him?

"Nobody made you gay, man," Darrin said in a voice that was soft, but still tough. "If anybody did, it was your goddamn father, not being around, leaving when you was three. See, James and me remember him. That's probably why you turned out that way."

That way. As if *that way* was the most horrible thing in the whole fucking wide world. Don't let them trap you into sentimental bullshit; they *hate* you. He looked at the gun. You got the power now.

"And what if Dad was the reason?" he said. "Was it so bad for me to be a fag? Did it really ruin your day that much?"

Darrin looked on the brink of an answer, but glanced at the gun and choked it back.

"Tell me." LeRon pointed the gun at Darrin, but Darrin held his lips tightly together. LeRon raised his thumb, ready to cock the trigger. "I said tell me."

"Hell, yeah, man. It was fucking embarrassing as hell. My friends used to come up to me and say, 'Is your brother a punk, man?'"

"And was that so bad, big brother?" High on the power, LeRon went into his Oprah imitation, the one his *girl*friends howled at. "Tell our studio audience and the folks at home; tell us, we're dying to know. Matter of fact, we're just dying, period. So tell us, why was it so bad for your younger brother to be such a goddamn, flaming, motherfucking-grade-A-queer-fucking-punk faggot—"

"'Cause nobody else had a brother that was a punk." Darrin looked ready to leap at him. "I tried to change you, man. I tried to make you a man, act rough with you, fight you, but you always went off and cried like a punk to Moma. Don't blame me, muthafucka, 'cause I tried. I didn't want no punk in the family."

"There you have it, folks." He held the gun as if the barrel were his microphone. "In the tough niggah world, being a punk is the ultimate fucked-up thing to be—" Suddenly all the muscles in his face tightened into one big ball. "Just ask any motherfucking asshole rapper." He pointed the gun to the poster of Big Daddy Kane.

"You like rap music," James said in their defense.

"Like hell," LeRon said, falling back into his own voice. "I *used* to like rap music. Now, every time I turn around I hear another rapper putting down gays in their lyrics. Shit like Salt 'n' Peppa calling us 'fruities.' All these fucking rappers talk about black pride and togetherness and positivity and education, but Big Daddy Kane writes a song talking about how he's anti-faggot and wants no homosexuality. You're all the same. You can't stand faggots, all you rappers and homeboys. Tone Loc, Young MC, Heavy D, Big Daddy Kane, and James and Darrin Davis — you're all the same, speaking in unison outta one big boom box. You don't give a damn about us, like we aren't a part of you, like we aren't black, just some fucking mutation of black, but not black, not worthy of being part of the race, not deserving of the pride and dignity you want all blacks to feel. You all call us fags; you all want us dead — like the Nazi youth movement wants Jews dead, like the Klan wants *all* blacks dead. Why? Why?"

For a second, nobody said anything. Then Darrin's eyes lit up as if he'd found the answer. "It's not right with God, and you know it."

"Oh, oh, excuse me," LeRon said, "but it's perfectly all right with God if you shoot up dope, sell crack, and father who knows how many babies that won't have a real daddy, huh? That's okay, huh? But having a dick slide up your ass to make you feel good isn't." He held up the gun like a microphone again. "Tell us, Darrin, have you ever tried having a dick slide up your ass? You might be surprised just how good it feels. Almost as good as that one isolated, but, oh, so memorable time when I was, oh, five or six and you were seven or eight and we climbed up in the top bunk of the bunk beds we had then and played with each other's—"

Darrin stood up fast. "Fuck you, man. You're going off, and I ain't gonna sit—"

LeRon popped up like Eastwood, like Bronson, like Schwarzenegger, his arms fully extended, the gun ready to go. "Sit your black ass down."

Darrin didn't move an inch, still ready to pounce.

LeRon flashed a cocky smile. "Go ahead, make a faggot's day."

Slowly, steadily, Darrin eased back onto his bed.

LeRon also sat, then turned to James with his Oprah voice. "And you, biggest brother of them all. How 'bout a few answers for our panel of judges. Like why you were always stealing my things, my clothes, my watches, my money. Why? Is it because you had this secret Freudian desire to *be me*? You never stole Darrin's things, just mine. Did you really want to be a sissyboy? Did you have a thing for me like I had for you?" He gave James a seductive nod and some sexy, girlish winks. "How 'bout it, big boy?" he taunted in a husky voice.

James stared back, too furious to speak.

"Let's jump him, man," Darrin said to James. "Get the gun away and call Moma to come take him to the hospital."

"Don't try it," LeRon commanded, his eyes still fixed on James.

"I'm sick of this shit," Darrin said.

James kept his stare and didn't respond.

"How 'bout it, big boy?" LeRon repeated.

"I'm getting sick of this shit," Darrin said.

"How 'bout it?" LeRon said again.

James's voice erupted. "Why were you always trying to feel my ass?"

"What?" Oh my God.

"You heard me. When I was in high school and you were around eleven. You were always trying to feel my ass when I was sleeping. Didn't think I knew what you were doing, huh? I knew, muthafucka, I knew. Every time I'd be sleeping I heard you tiptoeing around the room, sneaking up to my bed, trying not to put any pressure on the mattress. I felt your hand every time, first barely touching my ass, then running down it and all around my legs, and you were fucking beating off next to my bed."

LeRon sat there stunned, like when the doctor had told him about the infection.

"James, fuck that shit, man," Darrin said.

"Didn't think I knew about that, huh?" James said to LeRon. "Didn't think I knew."

"Fuck that shit," Darrin pleaded.

James stood up. "Who do I look like — yesterday's fool?"

"Get back." LeRon came out of his shock and stood up, too.

"I knew you were doing that shit." James came toward him. "Jacking your dick off as you were feeling my butt with your other hand."

"Get back." LeRon held up the gun, backing up slowly.

"Fuck this shit." Darrin stood up, too.

"Feeling your brother's ass — ask yourself who's sick." James kept coming.

"Get back, man, get back. Don't think I won't fucking blow your ass off the wall."

"Nobody *forced* you to do that, did they?" James kept getting closer. "Nobody forced you to feel my ass, sick boy."

"Man, *fuck* this shit." Darrin was jumping up and down.

"Huh, sick boy? I knew all along." James was right there now, towering over him, inches away from the barrel.

LeRon felt his heels, then the rest of the back of his body bump against the wall. "Yeah, you knew," he blurted out, "but you never said anything about it, big brother. Not one goddamn word. Why? Why? Was it because you liked it? You liked your little brother looking up to you and feeling you up, so you pretended to be asleep? Is that it? You liked me and wanted to have my stuff, and you liked it when your little brother got off on you. Tell our audience now, big brother."

"I'll fucking kill your ass," James said, shaking a finger so tight it looked like it was about to break off. There was something in his eyes, something LeRon had never seen before, something he couldn't place — fear, rage, murder, guilt. "You come in here blaming us for all your problems, for you dying, bringing all this shit up from childhood. Boy, that's just how it was. Nobody knew shit back then."

"I know you're not to blame. The world taught you being gay was sick. But I don't care. I don't give a fuck anymore. I gotta blame somebody. I'm sick and tired of all you niggahs calling us faggots, all you homeboy rappers."

"They don't *all* say that shit," Darrin said. "Me and James don't even talk about fags no more."

LeRon didn't take his eyes off James. "But you let others talk about your brother. You buy the albums. You support the prejudice when you go bopping down the street to Heavy D rapping about faggots being happy in jail. I hear that shit and how am I supposed to feel about the black community supporting me as a black man? I feel like they don't give a damn that I might be dying. You gotta stand up for me like you did when Manny Blake called me a fag when we were kids, only now you gotta say it louder. My life is at stake. My friends' lives are at stake. And when you don't stand up for me, you're just giving me one more thing to fight against."

"Give me the gun," James said, his hand inching up.

"I know you're not to blame. But it's gotta stop somehow. No matter who's right or wrong about faggots or whatever, do you really want your brother to die like this? Do you? Do you?" He cocked the chamber to force James back.

"Gimme the gun," James yelled.

"Don't pressure me. Think I'm weak? Think I'm not strong? How the fuck do you think I survived twenty-four years of your bullshit?"

"Man, give us the fucking gun," Darrin pleaded.

"Somebody's gotta pay." LeRon steadied his finger on the trigger.

"I'm taking the gun from you right now," James yelled.

"Somebody's gotta pay," LeRon yelled, ordering himself to shoot now, damn it. "Somebody's gotta fucking pay!"

"LeRon!" James yelled.

Eyes closed, finger ready to pull. Do it, damn it.

"LeRon," Darrin whispered.

"*Fuuuuuuuuck!*"

He felt the gun flying away from him, out of his hands, his insides yelling, *Get that fucking piece of death away from me.*

87

Glass crashed and shattered in his eardrums.

Only moments later, when he opened his blurry eyes and found himself on the floor, did he realize he had hurled the gun through the window, sending it crashing to the ground outside. He sat there, hunched over, the room all quiet.

"Shit," Darrin said with relief. "I'll get the gun," he said to James and ran outside. James just sat back down on the bed and wiped the sweat from his face.

The room was as still as the middle of the night.

"I'm such a pussy I can't even kill my own brothers," LeRon said.

"You ain't no pussy, boy." James got up and walked over to the window.

LeRon's breaths were coming in long steady huffs, but for the first time in hours he knew that he was actually breathing. His limbs felt limp, but they could move. His body was wound tight, but the blood was still running through. For the first time since he'd left the doctor's he felt: I'm still alive. Only then could he actually remember the morning that had led up to the afternoon.

"Coming out of the doctor's office this morning," he began, talking to himself as much as to James, "I was so confused and scared, like death was gonna come take me away any second. I was driving back to work. I couldn't even see the road straight, I was so much on the verge of crying. I was thinking how much I could really use a hug right then. Then I thought about one night when we were kids — I couldn't have been more than ten or eleven, and you were probably in your late teens. You stole five dollars out of my drawer, right in front of me. We fought about it, but you just knocked me down and said you needed it for Cherice. Remember you were dating Cherice back then?"

There was no answer as James continued to look out the window.

"Anyway," LeRon went on, staring at the floor, "when you came home that night I told you to keep the money, that I didn't want to fight anymore." He chuckled as he wiped the tears from his eyes. "I was eleven, and I didn't want to fight with my big brother anymore. I wanted to hug you. I wanted you to hug me — just a hug, just a big brotherly hug, safe and free, just a hug. I told you to keep the money if we could be friends again. You said okay and laughed like you thought what I was saying was cute. I was nervous as hell, but I wanted my hug. I reached up and closed my eyes and swung my arms around your shoulders and held on tight. I waited to see what you were going to do. Then I felt your arms around my back, your strong squeeze. You hugged me and I was okay. A few days later we were back to fighting again. Back to the war, and the hug was a casualty, forgotten until I remembered it this morning. I was driving and thinking I sure could use that hug right now. Then I heard Tone Loc on the radio, rapping about how he kicked a transvestite out of his house because this was the eighties and he was only messing around with the ladies, telling me eighties equals AIDS equals fags equals death. I couldn't take it anymore; I just couldn't take it. I just can't take it. I thought about all the times I've heard rappers put me down, then I thought about all the times you and Darrin put me down. That's when I decided to come here and get the gun."

He noticed James was at the phone now, dialing with his back to LeRon.

"Who you calling?" LeRon asked. "The police?"

"The police? Please—" James laughed like that was the craziest thing LeRon had said all day. "I'm calling Mom, man, calling Mom."

Robert Friedman · Bisonic ballet (pas de deux)

Nothing in my thirty-odd years as a delirious queen prepared me for Miranda, not even my briefing at Virgo House, my new "living situation." Julia, her biologic mom, took pains to make the point clear.

"We are a sharing house of fully independent adults: three dykes, one bisexual, and you—"

"Full-fledged fagface," I assured her.

"—yes, but we all have a stake in Miranda. You'll be expected to pitch in, get involved, not just, you know, feed her chocolate." Julia spoke in that firm, beautiful way self-assured dykes have. I was ready to die for Miranda. Yes, yes, I said, sign me up. It's been so long since I've had a home.

Over the course of the next few weeks, I got to know Miranda — cautiously, over breakfast. Miranda, if you are reading this (and I see you sitting on the great stained sofa in the kitchen, spilling crumbs and smearing jelly on these pages), know that you are privileged. Rarely has a great beauty been fictionalized so young, so forgive me if I paint in what you consider too broad a stroke. Miranda, of the wise jokes, of playground wisdom, of a thousand tiny gossips. Miranda, of the comic weariness of adults, their carnival pleasures: as befits the child of three mothers and two fathers. Miranda, born, not asked, into a hairy consensual household. Her chest is flat; her mind is round and alive.

Now, two weeks after our first meeting, I had the idea for the perfect icebreaker. I'd make it to her school by the final bell, catch Miranda on her way out, and we'd detour to the park on the way home. I got there minutes before that final, manic alarm, and, knowing that she had art last, tried to find the right wing. I had to trespass through the whole building to find it, and I had that very particular feeling you get when you walk down school halls as an adult, wading to your ribs in lockers which once seemed high as the doors to opportunity. The feeling has to do with being too old too suddenly.

I found the art room at the same moment that the bell sounded; the doors flew open, and I was standing in a flood of small humans, art projects spilling around my knees. I stood like a buoy and scanned the waves for the ponytail of Miranda. When the torrent became a trickle and still no Miranda, I ventured in, to root my little artist out. The room smelled of tempera paint and day care. Low formica tables were against the walls, midget chairs up-ended on them. Miranda was sitting in the only grounded chair, wrapped over a drawing. The art teacher, a young woman who must have had better places to be, was pretending to be busy over the paper cutter.

"I don't like to rush them when they're involved in a project," she whispered to me when I approached. "And this one is so intense."

"I know, she's mine," I told her, feeling like a father at P.T.A. I went over to her, leaning over in that intimidating adult way, and asked, "Whatcha drawing?"

She was startled, saw that it was only me, and relaxed.

"Hi, Stony. It's a picture of Julia." She handed me a picture of a woman in a large plaid skirt, with an even larger belly. Yes, this was Julia in her ninth month. She had a look on her face like she had just swallowed a volleyball. But why was she on all fours?

"No, you fluffhead, you're holding it wrong. She's on her back. I wanted to show how helpless she is, while she's producing this baby. I wanted to show all you men standing around, but plaid takes a long time."

"Standing around, ordering her to produce?"

"No, just standing around," Miranda said. "Feeble."

Miranda agreed to come along on my little outing because she thinks I look like a leading man on one of the soap operas she watches. She visits with her friend Tizzie, whose mother lets them sit in front of the TV, ogling the men on the soap operas. Miranda believes these men are important in her life; she is, in some ways, a sad child, precocious in tragic yearning. Julia doesn't know about the TV fests at Tizzie's.

I told Miranda I was taking her to see the buffalo in the park, whose existence she believes I made up. The park was lively and dripping with pleasures: boys like pretty tigers racing by on bicycles, roller skaters, joggers who ought to give up. I was happy to have Miranda to tease, and she seemed surprised with all the attention.

The buffalo grazed behind a wire fence in the center of the park. They are, after all the buildup I gave them, rather dreary animals. Their fur hung in clumps at their sides. Still, there they were.

Miranda said yuk. I said they reminded me of children. We stared at them for a while, getting a good whiff of their perfume. Soon Miranda tugged at my sleeve.

"Can we go, Stony? I'm tired of lugging my books, and I have to pee."

The trip did not seem an overwhelming success. By the time we got home, she was sulking, and all assumed she had just come from school.

But at dinner, when Sebastian (the bisexual; he won't wear a dress; another story) asked who had left hair in the bath and nobody owned up to it, I volunteered, "The buffalo," and Miranda brightened. No one asked, so it became a private joke between us, the whoopie cushion in any conversation. If one of the other adults did something dumb, like being an Authority Figure, and Miranda and I knew they were just buffalo, big and exotic but ultimately no big deal, we'd nod sadly, wisely to each other.

Soon Miranda was always asking: "Where are you going, Stony? Can I come, too?"

My life had become her field trip. Day after day, my adventures began to be noted. I tried to do the adult thing and ignore her: "I'm going out, just out." But I imagine even the Rock of Gibraltar must chip some at the edges, and eventually I succumbed to her interrogations.

"To my dance class. You can come if you can get into a leotard in the next thirty seconds."

"I don't have a leotard yet!" She was appalled at the stipulation.

"What are you waiting for? To grow breasts?" Although I knew the pleasure of gratuitous remarks, I was immediately sorry to have said this. "Okay, okay. I think Polly left hers drying in the bathroom." In fact, there it was, hanging shriveled on the curtain rod like a wet stretch sock. I slapped it, damp, on her back. "Hurry up or we'll be late."

"Why is it hot pink and shiny?" she asked. Miranda displayed the usual innocence of otherwise precocious children. In only a few years, while her peers were putting out for each other behind the art wing, Miranda would be reading everything at tenth-grade level, except the boys' eyes.

On the way, I leveled with her. "When I came to live at Virgo House, I never expected to have a sidekick. I never lived with a child before, you know, and now there's a fresh one on the way."

"I'm not a 'chi-uld,' I'm a kid," she said with that dignity you lose after adolescence. "You're a nice man, Stony, but you have this weird thing about children. You make us sound like eggs."

"Babies *are* like eggs, round outside, soft and dripping in."

"You stop saying those things about babies!" Miranda insisted. "I might one day want to keep mine!" She was a child of too many soap operas. Her remark reminded me that she was missing her daily genuflection on the altar of videogenic man. I, in turn, reminded her.

"That's okay, this is more fun than TV." This is when I knew I was in trouble. "Why do you take dance class? Will there be other kids? Do I look okay?" I am not sure where she got the idea that people are happiest when bombarded with questions — from "Donahue"?

"Wait till you see the sunset in the dance mirror. I take the late class because of the view." And it was almost true: the real reason I was taking dance class had nothing to do with sunset light. It was this: for two hours, a strong voice was telling me what to do with my body.

Miranda enjoyed the class, and Klaus, the teacher, was happy to have her attend. He told me to bring her again, because she added a "new energy" to the group. Miranda could do every exercise and stretched herself in ways I could only imagine. Sometimes I sat out an exercise by the wall.

After we had applauded Klaus and were collecting our things, a boy in the class named Theo walked over to us. Theo and I had slowly built up an acquaintance over many weeks, and I had noticed in recent days a new surge of friendliness on his part.

"You guys did well!" Theo said, not looking at Miranda. He was smiling at me. Blond hair fell like a check mark over his eyes. "You a team?"

"No," I said. Miranda, squeezing into the corner between us, was clearly thrilled he had come over. Life had topped TV again, and Theo looked like he merited a soap of his own.

"What's your name? Are you a real dancer? Why do *you* take this class?"

"I'm Theo. And *you* probably want to change up in the women's changing room. Did you know there was one?"

"No!" Miranda chirped, happy at last to be granted an adult environment. "I'll be back, Stony, after I've changed with the women."

"The reason I take this class," Theo continued after Miranda had left, "is all those mirrors. I can't help it, mirrors are like sex for me. A room with a wall full of mirrors is like a lot of sex."

It seemed that Theo had not stopped doing exercises.

"Want to come out for coffee?" he asked, just as Miranda reappeared in the mirror. I shrugged and pointed to her. When I remarked that her visit seemed swift, Miranda mumbled nonchalantly that she had not brought anything to change into. What a shame, I said, rolling my socks up calmly.

＊

I was dreaming of a forest overgrown with children. Theo, dressed in white, was having tea in a gazebo in the clearing beyond, and I was trapped in the thickets. Vines like Miranda's arms clamped my legs, and the trees were chorusing: "Tie your shoelaces!"

Julia tapped me awake. I had fallen asleep on the kitchen sofa.

"Thank you, it was pathetic."

"I wanted to talk to you about Miranda," Julia said, easing herself into her pregnancy rocker. "Ooof! I got a call from Ms. Scopes today."

"Who," I asked, "is Ms. Scopes?"

"Miranda's art teacher. It seems Miranda turned in her latest art proposal, a portrait of guess who?"

95

"I'm flattered."

"It seems you are clad in a leotard. Ms. Scopes said there was considerable attention paid to the physique. With you, engaged in what seems to be a *pas de deux*, is another man, with blond hair. In the background are what Ms. Scopes called 'very peculiar rats.' In all, a pretty picture of Miranda's home life!"

I shook my head confidently. "They are probably not rats, they're buffalo. Ballet with bison: what a festive idea."

"Ms. Scopes thought your pose was 'questionable.' She wants to know if you give permission for her to hang it on the sixth-grade bulletin board."

"Timid Ms. Scopes! Of course she can!"

"Miranda has certainly been full of you lately. It's 'Stony goes here' or 'Stony goes there.' I don't know why, but I think she has a crush on you."

"Well!" I said, raising myself from my slothful position. "You act as if there's nothing more outlandish! Hurrah, Ms. Scopes! Hang away!"

✳

Then Miranda decided I would like breakfast in bed. I opened my eyes, saying, "Theo," rolling over. But it was a little girl hand turning the doorknob. She walked in carrying a tray, her ponytail swinging.

"You're not allowed in here," I said, a lame threat. The door opened again, and Theo returned from the bathroom. He was wearing my bathrobe, which fit him better than it fit me. He looked like a Jim Dine canvas.

"Hi, Miranda, how are you? Hop in!" Theo climbed in so that she was between us. Miranda still held the breakfast tray tightly.

"Lucky there's enough for three," she said. "Raspberries in yogurt."

"Yeah!" said Theo. "Lucky there's all three of us here."

"You are not allowed in my room, little m," I reiterated.

"I know," she said, and then she started giggling. Theo joined in; I wanted them to stop. "I feel like I just crawled into the buffalo pen in the park and am having breakfast with the buffalo."

I looked at Theo and winced, but he didn't respond. By now, everyone in the house looked hostilely in my direction when Miranda started with the buffalo imagery. I made one last effort: "Children are not allowed here!"

"Then I'll have to leave!"

Miranda and I looked at Theo, who said this with his whole face: eyes wide, battleship grin.

"This is definitely better than cartoons at Tizzie's," Miranda said. "Sometimes around adults I feel like part of the house chores, but not with Stony."

"I know what you mean, Miranda, and I have only known him for a short time," said Theo. They were having a grand old time.

"No one thinks of you as a chore," he went on. "I am shocked."

"Not a chore," I agreed. "Merely a big responsibility."

"I remember dinners when there weren't enough chairs," Miranda said. "Or when I was too little for one. I sat in Julia's lap, always Julia's lap. Never once Sebastian's. Never once yours," she said to me.

"Did Sebastian ever let you sit in his bed and eat breakfast?"

"No," Miranda allowed. "This is true."

"And Stony does! You see, men aren't all that bad."

"Never mind Julia sometimes," I added.

"I have been thinking they are pretty feeble lately," Miranda confided to us. "Always wanting other people to tell them how to move."

"You'll get over it," Theo said. He squeezed her. Of course Theo was good with children — it came naturally, he being so close to a child himself.

"Miranda Liberation Day!" sang Theo, and soon Miranda was chiming in. "No longer a second-class citizen!"

"Have some raspberries and be quiet," I said, spooning some into her mouth. "People are still sleeping, children should be seen and *et cetera.*"

She glowered in my direction, slurping yogurt. She ponytailed me, turning to Theo. "How old are you?"

"I'm nineteen."

"So you're a big kid, but not compared to Stony."

"I know," he said.

She looked at him, at me, back at him. Something clicked in; slow, but still smart for her age. "I guess I'll go to Tizzie's," she said. "She's been real jealous of you, Stony."

"Of me?"

"Tizzie says you can only have one best friend, and who you spend Sunday morning watching cartoons with counts a lot."

"So true."

"We get in bed, too," she said, crawling out of ours, "to watch them."

She was at the door, and I said, "Miranda, remember to be back by five, for our dance class."

"Yeah," she said, posed at the threshold like some heartbreak farewell. "See you, Stony ... I love you!" She left.

Theo and I turned to our breakfast.

"I hope Tizzie's good at picking up the pieces. I think she's going to cry."

Theo blew steam from his tea. "I don't think I've ever been involved in a triangle with a twelve-year-old woman," he said. "Do I stand a chance?"

"We'll see if my tastes change," I said. "Adults can be such buffalo, you know."

✻

It was always like this with two lovers: quoting one to the other.

Carter Wilson ## The day Dick died

Dick and Jane were the offspring of violence and passion.

Jardin and Miguel's friend Grace brought the tale along when she came to deliver the puppies. Her own dog in those days was Tiffany, a sweet, diffident white-and-blue-gray Australian shepherd. Whenever Tiffany came into heat, males from all the mountains around Lompico were drawn to Grace's door. The only way to get any peace was to close Tiffany up in the abandoned trailer at the far end of the lot. But one time when Grace had to go to town for a few hours, a persistent, fierce young husky managed to gnaw through a corner of the plywood paneling, then ripped it aside enough to make a hole he could squeeze through. Of this union came seven, including Dick and Jane.

Dick had a long white-and-black coat and, even at six weeks, a big plume of tail. Jane's fur was short and coarse and yellow. Dick was careless, trusting, rambunctious. From the beginning, Jane always let him test the waters first. If they were invited into the house, Dick would charge right ahead, but Jane hung back until she could ascertain whether the climate inside was hospitable to dogs or whether Miguel was going to chase her around the dining room table whacking a newspaper against his hand.

At first the puppies stayed mainly outside on the deck. But at about ten weeks roaming began, larger and larger circles of inquiry up into the field beyond the house; then, when Jardin called, longer and longer pauses on their haunches before deciding whether they would come or not. Finally one Sunday Mrs. Strunk, a neighbor who hadn't said boo to either Miguel or Jardin in their first three years living on the hill, stalked down to complain about a sneaker she had just put through the washing machine and left to dry being stolen off her back porch.

Jardin cleaned out a little toolshed by the garage up under the house for Dick and Jane to sleep in at night. He hired a friend to sink the post holes for a 75-foot run the whole length of the bottom of the property, where the dogs could spend their days. He set the height of the wire fence at five feet. Dick and Jane were soon over and out. During Christmas, an old college pal and one-time lover visiting from Maine helped Jardin staple chicken wire over the top of the run. Dick and Jane discovered corners as the best places to fight their way through that. Jardin bought heavy-gauge galvanized wire for the top and placed two-by-fours at four-foot intervals to secure it. Dick and Jane took up digging. Jardin took to boarding up favored exits.

Even before he was fully mature, Dick's strength was a source of wonderment to Jardin. Pushing out boards with his muzzle, he could pop the heads off heavy nails. Jardin had to assume this was Dick, since the dogs did not work on their escapes when humans were in sight. Whether Jane provided the brains for the operation he couldn't tell. But he became convinced she was certainly an accomplice after one big break when the only way to reconstruct their m.o. was to assume Jane had stood for hours holding aside a length of rigid fencing wire with her teeth so Dick could squeeze in to dig at the boards behind it.

Angry as the escapes made him, Jardin also recognized them as games. The great rule, the rule of rules, appeared to be "Dogs always come back." Another, refined over time, was like the rule in human prisons: there must be, it seemed, an *interval* between breakouts. After a grand getaway, one involving extensive destruction, a long lull would ensue before the telltale scratching or the rubbed rawness on Dick's muzzle would begin again. Once when, out of disgust and despair and then preoccupation with other things, Jardin didn't even repair the latest rip in the fence, Dick and Jane went about their doggy lives inside for a month as though they had never heard there was any alternative to incarceration. The Saturday morning Jardin finally went down with his hammer and brads and nails and new boards, he first *invited* them to come out through their hole. Dogs pointedly looked the other way. Dogs decidedly not interested.

For an average escapade, they usually stayed gone about five hours. Dick was likely to reappear first, matted, dirty, tongue hanging out, tail waving and somehow, even in the dry summer months, soaking wet. Jane would hide out in the bushes to see what kind of reception Dick got. A warm welcome and she might come sidling up herself. But if it was kicks and curses for him, off she'd go again. Then she would hang out down on the road by the mailbox and bark wildly whenever a car or somebody on foot went by and make periodic forays up the driveway to yap herself hoarse beneath the window of the room where Miguel and Jardin slept. If Jardin got up, put on his robe, and went down, Jane would take off again.

A little too late for Dick and Jane (and for himself) Jardin bought a book called *Good Dog, Bad Dog*. It said if you could get your hands on your animal first, you could discipline it, but if it responded to a command, even at the last moment, the dog had to be praised. Everything from his own family training told Jardin this rule was wrong. He had been brought up to understand that real punishment must involve duration and the uncertainty of forgiveness. *(And you, Jardin, will just go to your room and stay there.* And if, with the sudden bright courage of the condemned, he sniveled, *How Long?* they would say, *Until we say you can come out.)* So it galled him when there was no other way to get hold of Dick and Jane except to say ever so sweetly, 'Come,' and then he had to act as though all was forgiven. As a result, he was inconsistent about punishment, and Jane's wait-and-see attitude made sense.

One of the upsetting things about dogs on the loose was how it complicated relations with the neighbors. At the time, Miguel and Jardin didn't know if there were any other gay people on their hillside, and Jardin thought it best to maintain a low profile. He was vulnerable to his neighbors, because he shared their belief in the first commandment of suburban neighborliness: "Keep your muck within your own boundaries." Having Dick and Jane made him less self-contained and more obvious than a proper bourgeois feels comfortable being.

Out on a walk, Jardin could *feel* how with nearly a hundred pounds of Dick and Jane at the ends of leashes he had become a being different — bigger and more complex — than Jardin alone. Jardin-with-dogs, for example, made sure that all other dogs kept an appropriate distance; correlatively, Bigger Jardin's idea of the proper way to greet other human beings involved more than a mere nod or grunt of hello; its notion of good manners included crotch-sniffing on first encounter, women as well as men. Jardin-with-dogs wanted to review the contents of each trash can the neighbors set out Thursday evening for the early Friday morning collection. Above all, the larger entity wanted to smell every dog turd on Elder Drive, old and new, and to leave some of its own in specific places on neighbors' lawns, preferably when the neighbors were peering out their windows.

Although he searched his Jardin-with-dogs heart, Jardin had no desire to shit on the neighbors. After a certain number of encounters with people on his block, however, he began to come around. The most righteous about the leash law, the quickest to bark, 'Can't you even control those animals, young man?' were the ones who let their own dogs out in the early morning to tip over garbage and deposit some fresh crap in the yards of their associates.

The other reason he became so upset when Dick and Jane got away was because of their woeful ignorance of consequence. They had never learned to stay shy of cars. Even Jane the Wary ran *toward* speeding vehicles. Both of them would taste anything they found lying on the ground, and would eat most of it. They did not know two dogs on their street, one of them their old white terrier friend, Pancho, had been poisoned. They could not read the notice posted on Judge Mahon's gate reminding people that killing dogs, even on your own property, is a felony, not a misdemeanor. Worst of all, Jardin could not get across to them what he had promised Miguel: that the first time they were picked up by the van from the animal shelter, he would pay the thirty dollars each to bail them out, but that they would get no second chance.

Dick and Jane were two years old before Jardin learned that all along they had been part of a grand design of Miguel's. "Way back in the beginning you said you wanted dogs," Miguel said, "and I thought they'd be good for you — get you out of the house, give you something to think about more than just me. We were getting too grown in on ourselves."

In other words, children. Jardin had never wanted any until he was thirty-five and fell in love with Miguel. Miguel could be quite militant on the subject. Why should heterosexuals with no demonstrable excess of affection to spare be allowed to adopt and he and Jardin, who loved each other so much, not? Jardin could see the point. In a world where biological parents let their five-year-olds out in the middle of the freeway at dawn, telling them to hang on to the cyclone fence until somebody comes for them, why should the plethora of emotion he and Miguel generated on Elder Drive — most of it good, all of it certainly intense — be made to go begging?

But not only the cliché of dogs as gay people's children made Jardin resist the idea of Dick and Jane being theirs. It was also the troublesome fact that his feelings for them were not one-hundred-percent loving, and his having screwed up their training and their having neuroses, and even the fact that neither of them had a prayer of ever getting into Harvard.

He continued wanting from them things they couldn't quite give him. In the area of training, for example: he imagined himself strolling out in the evening, seemingly alone. But then at his slight low whistle, four alert ears would prick from the underbrush and, with no hesitation, two magnificent beasts come bounding up and crouch at his heels, awaiting employment. Attempting to teach Dick and Jane this, Jardin began to see quite clearly how their shepherd and their husky ancestries were at war. Because the guy from the pound cruised their neighborhood in the morning, Jardin practiced off-leash training only at night. Let free at the foot of the driveway, Dick and Jane would heel tight in for a quarter mile down the road. Jardin would let them go with an "Okay" and they would sniff around, pee, come on command and nuzzle right up to the back of his left knee. They would make the turn at the redwood grove at the end of the street, heel again and come trotting back, all in a style their mother Tiffany would have applauded. But at the driveway, almost home, another deep masterly whistle would produce only tongue-hanging mad husky leers of good-bye and good luck as Dick and Jane slunk off to obey the call of the wild. Jardin was trying them off-leash one more time on an unusually warm August evening about nine o'clock when, at the far end of the road, without even a backward glance, Dick bounded off into a persnickety neighbor's garden and disappeared from sight. Jardin was not especially worried. He got Jane back on her leash and brought her home, fed her her heartworm pill and a bone-shaped biscuit, and put her in the pen under the house.

About eleven a man Miguel and Jardin knew only as Albert phoned and asked could he come by in a while. Jardin said it would be all right. Miguel, who had picked Albert up originally, but then lost interest in him, was not pleased. Albert worked as a live-in companion for a wealthy older man. He had been married a time or two and was, by his own lights, straight, although he told Jardin once maybe he thought maybe he was a little confused about his sexuality.

Albert had not shown by midnight, so Jardin and Miguel went to bed. An hour later a loud knock woke them, and Jardin went down. Albert was leaning on the door. He had been drinking. He got upstairs and got his clothes off and his furry long body into bed, but he didn't smell very clean.

Miguel decided to go down and spend the night in the guest room.

Jardin lay next to Albert playing with his penis. Albert kept saying, "Aren't you going to suck it? I thought you were going to suck on it." Jardin was saying again, very much as he would say when distant relatives asked him to come for the weekend, "I'd very much like to," when he heard barking outside. He put on his bathrobe, turned on a light, and went back down. Dick was at the top of the driveway, muddy, worn out, panting, tail wagging slowly. Jardin got him in the pen with Jane and double-latched the door and went back up to the discussion of whether or not he was going to suck Albert's penis.

A couple of minutes later Miguel stalked in and announced, "Your dogs are trying to break down their pen," and stalked out again.

"I heard them," Jardin called after him.

The pen was made of open slats. Thumping and wrestling around in the night were fairly standard, but Jardin had learned the frantic battering he heard now was the sign the dogs had diarrhea and really needed out. He got up again and put on pants and a shirt and went downstairs.

As soon as he pulled the bolts, Jane pushed out between his legs and took off. Dick lay shaking on the cement, his body extended, back legs caught under the pallet he and Jane slept on. Jardin got the pallet lifted and dragged Dick outside. The dog was rigid, silent.

Jardin went in to the guest room and, without turning on the light, told Miguel, "He just lies there and twitches."

Miguel said, "Then why don't you tell him to get up and go home?"

Jardin called 911, the emergency number. The woman there said to call a veterinarian. At the animal hospital he got an answering service and then, after a long pause and a transfer, the sleepy voice of his own vet, Dr. Bauman, who happened to be on call. Jardin told him Dick smelled bad and he was breathing and shaking, but otherwise he couldn't move anymore. It didn't appear he had been hit by a car, there wasn't any blood.

"Better bring him on down then," Dr. Bauman said. "How long will it take you to get here?"

"About ten minutes," Jardin said. He looked at the clock on the oven. It was a little after two a.m.

"I'll meet you," Dr. Bauman said.

Miguel ran to get his clothes on and to tell Albert they were going.

Jardin got his arms under Dick and lifted. He was very still. As Jardin was carrying him across to the car, a single long thrill like an electric shock ran through him and then suddenly he became much heavier. Jardin put Dick in the backseat. When Miguel got in, Jardin told him he thought Dick was dead. But once on the freeway he still pushed seventy-five, then eighty.

"I didn't know when we got them," he said, "but if we wanted to have Dick and Jane for our dogs, we should have lived in the country."

Miguel rested his hand on Jardin's leg.

"But under the circumstances, I guess they did as well as they could," Jardin said. "Friendly dogs. People liked them."

"Your doing," Miguel said.

At the vet's, there was one light burning inside and a single beat-up old Mercedes in the parking lot. Dr. Bauman carried Dick in and put him up on the steel examining table. The doctor was wearing a pajama top out over pants and flip-flops and had not combed his hair. Jardin apologized for getting him up. Dr. Bauman said, "Well, as long as there was a chance—" Then, more vaguely, "—if we'd gotten to him a half hour sooner—" He unfastened Dick's collar and took it off. "Want to keep this?"

Jardin said no, then yes, he would. He took the collar and shoved it down into his back pocket.

Gopher-Get, Dr. Bauman thought. The pellets looked like dry dog food, and some people didn't bother covering the stuff up enough to keep animals from getting at it.

Jardin brought up the two poisonings on Elder Drive. Bauman said he *could* perform an autopsy and probably get an answer, but it would cost some, and his own feeling was always when he could he'd rather go on believing it was an accident. Then you didn't have to think of your neighbors being as evil as that.

Jardin looked at Miguel, who only shook his head. "Okay, no autopsy then," Jardin said, siding with the doctor and against his own impulse.

Kelly McQuain
The escape velocity

Driving to the moon is possible in a man's lifetime. My Volkswagen Beetle has seen better days, but even so it's driven almost 120,000 miles and is still going strong. This is the car that Jerry Bishop took up through Canada, to Alaska, and down through California before driving it back to West Virginia. That's where he sold it to me. Cheap. One hundred twenty thousand miles on this car alone, half the distance from the earth to the moon, clocked up on cross-country trips like that. And if one car can see that much country, you just think for a minute how many miles it is a man drives in his lifetime, and you'll be surprised, I bet, to see how he could quite easily drive all the way to the moon by the time he is forty, forty-five. I tell this to Robert, and he looks at me out of the corner of his eye like I'm crazy or something. "You and your useless facts," he says.

※

Lazy lady sits fat in the sky, hands across her belly, torch song upon her lips: *That's amore,* she sings, and young lovers swoon by the edge of the harbor. Weak in the knees, a moonlight kiss. From the roof we can hear the traffic of the street, we can see that harvest moon hanging low in the sky, touching the tops of distant buildings.

"In West Virginia it's so dark, Rob. No city lights. You really see those stars, you really see that moon." When I was eleven, I got a telescope for Christmas. I put it together from a box, a young Galileo looking up, looking out, looking over those mountains at that vast escape called space. The final frontier. A five-year mission with Vulcans and phasers, beam me up and out, Scotty. Beam me up and out. I got as far as Philadelphia.

Galileo, telescope. I read about the period when he concerned himself, almost exclusively, with falling bodies. Well, the bodies I concern myself with these days are an entirely different matter. I've become Copernicus now, advocating a heliocentric model of human relationships.

"Kiss me," I say, and with reluctance Robert slides his hands out of his pockets and walks to me, pacifies. I find it rude when he walks back to his original position on the roof.

※

We take for granted that she has a back, although we never see it. She rotates her fat body, keeping pace with the earth, always showing only one face as if to say, I'm content, I'm happy. This is enough. Her cycle to spin around on her axis matches exactly the time it takes her to spin around the earth. Twenty-seven days — a bit over, actually. I was amazed when Mrs. Brohman had our science class use direct observation to find this to be true. I kept a careful record the whole month of February, had a science project called "The Moon Is Our Friend." Yes, the same face always stares at the earth, the same face. How would you feel if someone looked at you all the time with that same stupid face? I imagine Robert saying this.

That's not the way it is, not the way at all. Her face changes, don't you see? She waxes and wanes, she hides her face with the fan of night. "The way she works," I told him, "is like this: a simple explanation where the phases relate to the position of the sun and moon in the sky, as seen from the earth. As the moon orbits around the earth, the angular distance from which we view the moon changes, allowing us to see more, then less, of the side of the moon that is illuminated by the sun. The time it takes for a complete cycle of phases, a lunar month, is twenty-nine point five days." (Thank you, Mrs. Brohman.)

"But what is it you really see when you look at it?" Robert asks. He stands awfully close to the edge of the roof, looking up, looking careless.

"I don't know," I say, thinking. "I see a rough, raw diamond."

"Rough like you," he tells me, lightly gripping my shoulders from behind. He only touches me when he wants to touch me, not when I need to be touched. Yes, and she's trapped in a revolution around this planet. I see craters and mountains and vast seas of dust; maybe once she had a life of her own, but now — now her brilliance is reflected glory. Patient moon, measuring off time in your devotion. "Galileo determined the height of the moon's mountains by measuring their shadow—"

"Oh, for chrissake. Be quiet and enjoy it." His lips run across the back of my neck. I turn around, lay my open hand against his cheek.

"What's this?" I ask.

"Forgot to shave."

"I thought you were turning into a werewolf."

"I'm cold," he says. "Let's go back down."

✳

Moonlight, moving over your moving form, moving, moving. Moving over me. Ahhh, alive with pleasure, the man says in those ads. This is our futon, these are our blankets, that is our dresser, and our window. It amazes me that after two years the sex can still be so good.

A long time ago I told my friends I was in love with your weight, and they didn't know what I meant. Your weight, not physically but psychically, that innate pull, that sense of presence. Since then I've learned the equations that govern the rules of attraction, why I still stand around you in the kitchen when it's your turn to fix dinner. I know it's the mass of two objects that pulls them toward each other. You're bigger than me, you weigh more, so it was only natural that I got caught in your field instead of the other way around. For two whole years I've circled around you, through the apogee and perigee of fighting and making up, trying to wear the same contented face. But like the moon I no longer have an atmosphere of my own; I cannot breathe.

And now I know there exists a minimum speed needed to escape my orbit.

David Watmough

Eurydice, may I kiss the cop?

He was slim, dainty, and a blond, but even from the third story, one could tell that peroxide had a lot to do with that. Ken first noticed him down on the lawn, from our living room window, when the U-Haul truck was parked outside Century Apartments. My roommate observed that, with the beginning of the month, the rentals were once more changing.

"My God! Look at this!" Ken called out to me in the bathroom, where I was attending to my regular Saturday morning chore of cleaning my comb. "You should just see what is moving in!"

I joined him at the window as a young man in white shirt, pants, and seersucker jacket supervised the unloading by wildly gesticulating his arms and tossing the bright gold mane. Whether he was yelling in concert with his almost balletic movements, we couldn't be sure from behind the glass pane.

Not that his motions seemed to matter, as the two guys doing the actual unloading largely ignored him. Shortly, he was joined on our miserable patch of summer-ravaged grass by someone more like himself than the butch-looking workers.

"Who do you think *that* is?" Ken asked. "A roommate?"

"They're wearing matching seersucker jackets," I observed. "They *must* be lovers."

Ken would have no such generalization. Then he was a university professor of French literature, and I but a junior journalist whose stories dealt much in stereotype or, as my lover reprovingly told me, cliché.

"They probably went to the same sale. September is a month when stores unload such summer stuff cheaply." He paused. "But you may be right, Davey. There's certainly something a little Tweedledum-Tweedledee about them."

"That could be because they're faggots. Look how they both put their hands on their hips when they're not waving them about."

"There you go again with your generalizations. So they're a shade more effeminate than us. That makes them neither nelly queens nor ardent lovers. All the same, I wish blondie wouldn't *sway* so much. Oh, now he's grabbed the other's hand!"

"I must say this is exciting, Ken. Better than watching the Christian Scientists move in," I said, referring to a couple in late middle age who'd taken the apartment next to ours. The woman had appeared to be suffering from a major disorder, she looked so pale and frail. One day in the elevator, her husband told us that they had moved from a house to an apartment because she could no longer climb stairs. They had searched unsuccessfully all over Fort Lee for a ground-floor rental and had only taken the one in Century because of the elevator.

As the two stocky men struggled with a Victorian chaise longue up to the entrance, the blond youth darted into the van and emerged with what looked like an ornate brass monstrance between his hands. Prancing in their wake, he

113

held it up and waved it from side to side — as if blessing a church congregation with the glassed-in Host.

I was a little shocked at this quasi-blasphemous action. Nor was I reassured when he was followed by his friend carrying a large crucifix that he had also extracted from the U-Haul. At least he didn't wave it in benediction. I noticed him stagger, but that could've been because it was so heavy.

"Maybe they're gay, maybe they are lovers; they certainly seem to be religious nuts. What on earth do you think they've got all that ecclesiastical bric-a-brac for?" I asked my roommate.

"I don't know — but we might accidentally end up down there in the hallway with them and find out. Let's go."

This was so uncharacteristic of Ken that I stared at him as if he'd gone crazy. "You mean right now?"

"Well, I've no desire to knock on their door and ask why they need a monstrance and huge crucifix in their apartment. If we're going to be nosy we might at least be discreet about it."

I was dying to find out, of course. Then I was the inquisitive one. Ken usually let knowledge of neighbors come to him — which it invariably did. I was at the front door before he'd left the window space. Even so, I waited. "What kind of excuse can we use to find out?" I asked him excitedly, as he closed the door.

He gave me a playful punch to the arm as we reached the top of the stairs. "You'll think of something. You always have in the past." I think he was going to elaborate, but was put off by the sight of two dark-suited, solemn men — who I was sure were Christian Science visitors — waiting to be let into the apartment of our sick neighbor lady. In any event, they ignored us entirely.

When we got downstairs a lot of *adieus* were going on. The lads who'd done the really tough work were leaving and receiving the effusive thanks of our new fellow dwellers in Century Apartments.

Blondie's voice rose above all others, so shrill that I was surprised we had not heard what he was saying from our living room. "Tad and Andreas, you guys are both beautiful. We'll never forget your kindness! Thanks for the beautiful truck, for giving up your beautiful Saturday for us and coming all the way across the Hudson from beautiful Columbia Heights just to help us move into this dump. You sure you won't stay and have something to eat? Not even a drink?"

The shorter one smiled and shook his head. "That's nice of you to ask, Dan, but Tad and I must get back. By the time we return the U-Haul it will be midafternoon. And then we've got to get all dressed up. We're going to Sardi's tonight."

"It'll be a real drag," added the taller Tad. "But we can't get out of it. Dad and Mom want us to meet sister Olga's prospective in-laws. One of those boring family affairs."

"Andreas, I'll never say a bad word about premed students again," said Dan. "And I am glad, Tadeusz, you decided to take that course in American Lit with me. Could you imagine Eurydice and I trying to drive that huge thing down here to Fort Lee from Columbia — let alone load and unload it? The Kucharski brothers have saved our lives. God bless you, my dear children. And may He also bless that saintly Polish psychiatrist who sired you and whom I'm booked to see next week at the Medical Center. You might remind him Tadeusz, darling!"

Smiling, the brothers pushed their way stolidly backwards through the swing doors. Blond Daniel and brunette Eurydice turned and faced the two of us hovering at the foot of the stairs.

Daniel was unabashed, although I thought it obvious that we were eavesdropping. "Such darling boys, don't you think?" he said. "You heard how kind they've been to their dowdy sisters? By the way, I'm Daniel Corrigan and this silent faun is Alan Borrell — far better known, though, as Eurydice Resurrexit."

Ken — again surprisingly — stepped forward with outstretched hand. "Welcome to a considerably-less-than-new Century," he said. "I am Ken Bradley and this is my roommate, Davey Bryant. We saw you bringing your stuff in and were fascinated by that monstrance. And the cross you were carrying," he said, addressing Alan alias Eurydice.

My lover wasn't usually shy, but he simply didn't come on so breezily with absolute strangers. Consequently, I stayed as quiet as Alan and visually summed up the two of them as Ken extracted further information from a voluble Daniel.

The latter was not physical perfection, but with pale blue eyes, the flowing gold locks, and delicate features above that wiry, energy-charged body, he was indubitably striking. His roommate had a swart appeal of his own. Alan was slightly taller, equally slim, and possessed of dark, glittering eyes that I immediately found attractive. And as a chatterbox myself, I do not doubt I found his more-silent composure as much a magnet as I perceived Daniel's endless sprays of ornate speech a trifle daunting.

From Ken's casual questions I learned they were both grad students at Columbia, and both from the same small town in Pennsylvania. Daniel was a major in art history and wrote poetry, which was being published; Alan was pursuing a Ph.D. in classics, in which he preferred Greek to Latin.

The last item was learned amid the chaos of scattered furniture and goods in their new apartment on the second floor, where we had reluctantly adjourned while they both cast around for both glasses and the makings of a drink.

Ken and I sat on the chaise longue — the chairs were all piled high with books — just like ours, for the living rooms were replicas — as our hosts bobbed about in a miniscule kitchen that was also a duplicate of ours one floor above.

We didn't learn any more then — except, perhaps how utterly impracticable they both were. For, as we had both anticipated when reluctantly agreeing to join them for a drink before they'd had time to settle in, the invitation had turned into a minor social disaster. Twice I fled upstairs during our relatively brief stay: the first time because they couldn't find a third glass; the second for mix, as they'd run out of Canada Dry and had no tonic.

The inconveniences didn't faze either of them. My return was greeted with screams of joy from Daniel, who appeared to be in even better spirits than when I'd departed. Our poet neighbor and his classicist mate were circulating what looked like a grubby homemade cigarette but which we were informed was a variety of marijuana. They offered me the short stub, but, like my roommate in my absence, I prudently refused. At the time neither of us had the faintest inkling of what marijuana was all about; nor did we then suspect that the pharmaceutical avant-garde had that day moved into Century Apartments.

Back in the decorous order of our own place, we were distinctly aware of a clock-ticking quiet. In the course of the evening Ken more than once laughed out loud at something the mercuric Daniel had said. On the strength of that I allowed as to how charming I'd found Alan. Before going to sleep that night we both expressed the hope we would see more of the boys in the future. That in itself was a departure, as we had long ago agreed to keep to ourselves and not socialize with other people in the building.

A week elapsed before we invited Daniel and Alan up to dinner, ostensibly to listen to a Caedmon record of Dylan Thomas that Daniel had mentioned as loving but not owning. Ken and I were determined to entertain them properly so that we could get to know them better and at leisure. That initial encounter had been so fragmented, not to say hysterical. With all that in mind we not only decided to restrict the meal to the four of us, but Ken bought a leg of lamb — the roasting of which would give him, as cook, the maximum amount of time with our guests.

That Saturday evening forced me to acknowledge just how formal and conventional Ken and I were. Whether we'd started out that way or gradually developed as such while pursuing our burgeoning careers — me in the city, Ken on campus — I couldn't be sure. Hindsight tells me that it was not so much a flash of self-knowledge that revealed us as a somewhat stodgy and conservative pair but the heady contrast of the freewheeling style of the Columbia couple, who seemed not so much emancipated from bourgeois restraint as unaware of its existence.

We hadn't gotten through an initial round of cocktails before my sense of propriety received a severe buffeting from Daniel on the subject of his sex life and, by extension, on the subject of mine. He had draped himself elegantly around the end of our long sofa, sitting on one leather-panted leg with the other extended to reveal magenta hose and tasseled loafers. He was wearing a black billow-sleeved shirt that appeared to be made of lace and was accented by a flimsy silk scarf that was the same color as his socks. His profusion of blond hair cascading to his shoulders created a bizarrely biblical look.

Alternatively, Alan — with a couple of modifications — could have stepped off the *Mayflower*. Although he, too, was attired in pants and shirt of basic black, his apparel was offset by a large white 'Peter Pan' collar and a white sash in lieu of a belt. However, the similarity ceased abruptly at that sartorial level. As on the first day, Alan was as con-strained as his partner was ebullient.

"I blew the most perfect ten-inch black dick I've ever tasted at Neddick's — forgive the pun — in the Village," Daniel announced, as he sipped his first martini, thus sparking my aforementioned prudery. "Are you into black meat, Davey? Or are you a 'fellatio-racist' like Eurydice?" This query, because my erotic instincts were indeed stirred by black America, filled me with confusion and caused me to blush sufficiently for even my roommate to comment. "Davey doesn't like to spell these things out, but I bet it isn't long before he pays a lunchtime visit to Neddick's from his midtown office!"

Only Alan took pity on me and tried to change the subject. "I wish he wouldn't call me Eurydice. He says it's because I hate snakes and the lady was supposed to have died from one. But I think it is only because he wants to use me as a woman."

"Eurydice, my darling, it has nothing to do with the beauty of your bottom. It is indeed because you share a hatred of snakes with the wife of Orpheus. I never forget she was bitten by a serpent while being pursued by Aristaeus, who was an apiarist. I also adore bees and love nothing more than to lie naked in the purple heather of Scotland and have hundreds of them alight on my tool."

That brought momentary silence. Ken broke it as he fetched anchovy paste canapés from the kitchen. "So you know Scotland. I've never been there."

"Alas, only through the pages of Sir Walter Scott," Daniel exclaimed. "Particularly his masterpieces, 'The Two Drovers' and 'The Highland Widow.' I get a hard-on whenever I read either of those marvelous short stories. Does great literature make *you* tumescent?" he asked Ken.

Again, Alan diverted such frontal attacks. "I wish you would call me Ganymede," he said with an endearing pout. "That embraces so much more of me than that silly bitch who got stuck in Hades because her husband was a dirty old man who had to peek!"

Ken and I burst out laughing. We were unused to such campy treatment of classical myths.

Daniel was not about to have attention wrested from his more carnal contributions to the conversation. Yet however embarrassing, bracing as an ice-cold shower, and startling in its vigorous shoving of thought and emotion to realms hitherto regarded by Ken and me as unimaginable socially, all was good-natured and launched in the highest as well as the wildest of spirits.

"...I believe that masturbation is the most seriously undertaught practice in our school system today. It is left to the callow conventions of the locker room — and even worse, furtive self-discovery — when there is a Pandora's box of pleasure waiting to be opened by two hands and every male body.

"...No poet should be allowed admittance to the American Academy of Arts and Sciences until he or she has demonstrated mastery of the pornographic poem. From Blake to Auden — and I guess everyone's read his blow-job poem by now — there is proof of that.

"...I am personally composing an 'Ode to the Uncut Cock' but need to do more research. I won't even ask Ken, as he's from California, and the scalpels have been busy mutilating male meat all across this continent for years. All we have are a few black pricks that have remained *au naturel* — and they're from the primitive Deep South! But you're from Europe, Davey. Did the knife-happy surgeons leave you alone at birth? I gather you're not Jewish?"

I drew in a lot of breath and offered a rictus rather than a proper smile. "I am Gentile and uncircumcised, Daniel. I gather you are too?"

Which brought a reproving finger wagging at me. "Cunning creature! You want me to reveal all! And so early in our relationship! You must be patient. This is just *tell* time, isn't it, Ken?"

"It's almost *dinner*time," said Ken. "And I must say all this talk about meat is making me *very* hungry!"

Once more I threw my lover a look. I had the odd feeling that if dinner hadn't loomed at that moment we might indeed have been looking at one another's genital equip-

120

ment. I was distinctly anticipating the aftermath when we'd left the restriction of the table and had the rest of the evening to play with.

Daniel's infinite medley of moods determined a somewhat different outcome. The four of us were no sooner sitting once more on the sofa and chairs when his rather sharp features contracted, and he curtly announced the onslaught of a headache.

"I hope it was nothing we've given you to eat," said Ken politely. But by the apprehension that appeared on Alan's face I knew this was nothing to do with indigestion.

I jumped to my feet. "Let me get you an aspirin and water. I know how shitty headaches can be."

Daniel stared at me. For a weird moment I had the impression he didn't even realize I was standing there. He folded his arms tightly about his thin form and rocked ever so gently. His face was now pale; only his lips interrupted a sea of white with their carmine gash.

Alan spoke on his behalf. "He has his own medication. Here, Daniel, you should've taken this before you came up." He handed his friend a dark blue cylindrical pill from a small leather purse.

"Would he like a glass of water with it?" Daniel's totally abstracted look made me talk as if he were not in the room with us.

Alan grimaced. "He's used to taking them any time. It could be up the Empire State Building, or when he's got them rolling in the aisles during class."

As Daniel popped the thing in his mouth, he visibly relaxed; his arms came down from clasping his sides. I wondered momentarily at the medicine's instantaneous effect — then privately rebuked myself for being so naive. Obviously the physical action of recourse to the pill reassured him. His ensuing conversation confirmed it.

"Don't look so alarmed, Davey. It'll go in a few minutes, now. Mind you, I shall feel like an Irish armpit later."

Ken smiled wanly. "What does an Irish armpit feel like?"

Daniel bestowed him a soft look, a gentler expression than I had seen on those mobile features since they had arrived that evening. "You really wouldn't want to know, sweetheart. At least not from this Son of Erin tonight."

That was the first time that Daniel referred to his Irish background. But no mere Hibernian ancestors provided the substance of his subsequent revelations. The socially pusillanimous me of that period rather wished they had. Instead he told of horrors behind that aborted headache and the others that had so frequently plagued him.

While he vividly described his mental ordeals, he clung determinedly to that banter which was obviously his proven armor against the assault of hobgoblins. He insisted we view him as a kind of Ophelia, only more delicate and not given to collecting weeds from his garden. Very rarely did he suit expression and gesture to his nightmare tale of attempted suicides and incarcerations in state mental institutions.

With ringing of hard laughter, he described his rape by a guard with a lazy eyelid and a curved cock in one such asylum. He told of demented patients on neighboring beds, busily picking out stitches earned from jumping from third- and fourth-floor windows. And when Alan tried to restrain his torrential spewing, he perversely insisted on providing us with a detailed description of the third occasion he'd attempted suicide. He had resorted to wrist slashing in a warm bath. His roommate, hearing no sound of lapping water through the closed bathroom door, had rushed in and saved him.

At one point in this saga of the raw nerve ends and emotional turmoil of our visitor, I looked about the living room of the apartment. Our fittings and furniture had never been exposed to such starkly drawn images of insanity. I grew restless in my armchair. Daniel's unsettling narrative seemed never-ending as the hour grew late.

122

But the tale concluded as abruptly as he'd received the visitation of the headache. One moment he was describing a male nurse in Riverdale who had grabbed his long hair and forced him with a metal spoon to open clenched teeth and swallow some sedative to shut him up. Next, he was telling us that when he and Alan first met — while cruising the men's john on the Times Square shuttle — they had gone directly to a hotel and not gotten out of bed for two days.

Mercifully, Alan took this as a cue. "I think it's time I got this one back into bed with me," he announced, "Only it won't be for forty-eight hours, I assure you. We both have term papers to deliver on Monday, and neither of us is finished."

The sudden intrusion of such domestic detail came with the shock of cold water to the face. I shuddered and drew deep breath, clambering unsteadily to my feet in concert with our guests.

Ken and I made swift eye contact as Daniel compliantly let Alan pivot him around to face the door. All the demonic fire seemed to have fled as he smiled sweetly at us prior to being led downstairs by his solicitous lover. I surmised that all the spewing talk had proved its own catharsis — cleansing him momentarily of madness and restoring him to that thin tightrope of sanity on which he had to walk so precariously when the headache alarm bells clanged to threaten his elusive balance.

Ken demonstrated a similar awareness by clutching me with unusual fervor when we clambered into bed. I think we were both truly afraid of that sudden glimpse into Daniel's unholy night.

✻

We didn't see the pair for a full month after they had called to thank us and apologize for staying so late. By the time we received a return invitation, the graphics of that initial dinner party had dulled, and we were once more enthusiastic about seeing them. As Ken put it, it was as if our exotic neighbors inhabited not merely a whole floor below us, but a different and distinctly more exciting universe.

Both of us took more care than usual with our appearance. Not so much with clothes — in the bourgeois custom of the era we wore the standard Brooks Bros. button-down shirts, chinos, loafers. But Ken had taken extra care with the ironing of the Oxford shirts, and I had ducked into Altman's one lunchtime after the visit had been proposed and purchased an expensive bottle of after-shave for Ken and a phial of men's cologne for me.

I was to be glad I did — but not for any reason I could have concluded prior to our freshly bathed and carefully combed appearance at the front door of the two grad students from Columbia.

Daniel and Alan's selection of aperitifs was minimal — vodka neat, vodka with tonic, or vodka with water. Daniel did mention Cointreau as an alternative mix, but cautioned that he had once passed out from the combination. He also hinted he would rather keep that as an after-dinner beverage. We three readily agreed.

The meal, which we took in the kitchen, consisted of Swiss fondue. As Ken and I had never partaken of it before, our hosts volunteered to initiate us into the skill of spearing and safely extracting small cubes of beef from the bubbling oil in the chafing dish. We each selected a partner. I had the quiet, dexterous Alan, and Ken had an enthusiastic Daniel, who leaped at his morsels of meat with the soaring gestures of a faun.

Whether we visitors were already impaired by the prodigious amounts of vodka consumed before we reached the table, or whether we subconsciously welcomed the close tutelage of our hosts, I still find hard to specify. But the inevitable result was a proximity as intimate as tango dancers' — as their hands clasped the back of ours, heads drew close, and we were gently guided toward our culinary targets. At that moment Alan commented on the fetching fragrance of my eau-de-cologne as his nose nuzzled my ear.

When my shoulders were squeezed in the compass of his arms against his chest, I knew total relaxation. By the time his tongue found my mouth, my face was already lifted in supplication. I forgot the food; forgot everything except this new and questing body melting into mine. *Almost* forgot. Guiltily, I flashed a look over Alan's embracing arm to Ken sitting across the kitchen table. Something along the lines of what I was experiencing with Alan was being duplicated across the room between Daniel and my lover.

Shocked, yet immobile, I watched the sinuous Daniel slide onto Ken's lap and slowly unbutton that carefully ironed Oxford shirt. As if in some wordless, celluloid sequence, my roommate and the lad in his lap divested each other of garments. Finally, the entwined couple pushed away from the table, and Daniel's bare haunches filled my sight.

Before the two of them had turned sufficiently for me to see the degree of their mutual arousal, the hand that had guided mine to the fondue now quested me. With swift dexterity, Alan unzipped my slacks, deflecting my attention from the writhing across the table and — via his sweet lavishing of fingers and mouth — focusing it on the alternate ends of my own quickening body.

From either above me or from across the formica expanse I heard the hissed plea: "Let's go to bed." I was now all pliancy, open to every entreaty. With his left arm about my shoulder, his right hand tightly embracing my hard cock, my companion escorted me, now nude, from the kitchen toward the apartment's only bedroom. There was no haste; in fact, the procession was almost stately as he led me by my throbbing penis down the hallway.

With my sight blurred in erotic longing, for I now had my hand lovingly encircling Alan's engorged member, I noticed the other couple had already responded to the invitation of the pulled-back sheets.

The next moment we were a tangle of cocks and mouths, thighs and buttocks, balls and anuses, in a licking, panting sexual mosaic. For the first and last time in my life there were six balls to taste and caress in succession, three jerking rods eager for fleshly encounter with the half-dozen moist and dry entrances of a trinity of ever-writhing bodies. The dizzying pleasure of moving from the beloved familiarity of my Ken's satin flesh to the foreign allure of Daniel's dark pubic bush and the pink insistence of Daniel's huge mushroom-headed phallus became a delirium all its own.

For me, until the moment of that inebriated evening — for without the drink I am sure Ken's and my inhibitions would never have been vanquished — orgy had spelled *bacchanal,* or debauchery among a dissolute elite. That moment on the bed, under the sure and eager tutelage of our excitable poet, for it was Daniel, not Alan, who was the sure choreographer of our intricate sexual congress, became a final emancipation from the thrall of prudery.

How long we explored I cannot recall. I do know that the explosion of quadruple ejaculations, as semen flowed into and across our panting bodies, was virtually simultaneous. I also remember there were smiles on four faces when eyes finally met as we slowly and stickily reached parallel positions on the rumpled bed.

There was no resting and then repeating of the performance, but all four of us slept together that night. The quartet did not rise for a jolly breakfast, but rather Ken and I stole away at the time the milkman used to be on his way.

I cannot say that after that extraordinary transfer from the table to the bed, the four of us settled down to become good friends and apartment mates.

There was a sequel to those first three encounters, but the fourth and final one had nothing of the muzzy euphoria and sheer frenzy of passion when we had know each other as such a fiercely erotic quartet.

Repetition was what we sought, though; Ken and I planned for it. For after, rightly or wrongly, assuring one another that what had happened was only incidental to our relationship and didn't threaten our mutual fidelity, we prepared for another dinner party, which would hopefully lead to bed for the four — but without the aid of alcohol or even fondue. I think we also discussed — while laughing like titillated schoolgirls — the possibility of changing initial partners, so that I would glide off with our poet, while Ken would escort the classics scholar to a joint assignation on the king-size mattress, which we decided to sprinkle with the miniscule ears of fresh lavender.

None of this was destined to happen. Nor in the light of what did occur was it ever again feasible — or even desirable. The events were thus. A month at least had gone by since our four-way sex. There had been quick hellos in the foyer since we had become so unconventionally intimate, but no real talk, not even phone conversation. Then, at three o'clock, one dark and rainy November morning, we both woke on our unscented bed and gaped at each other.

We had been awakened by a scream. Before we had time to exchange words there was another. And another. By now we were out of bed, in our robes, and darting for the door. We did not recognize Daniel's voice, so shrill and inhuman was the sound. But we knew the source of that plaintive terror. Hadn't its owner prepared us himself in his graphic and detailed evocation of one of those frightening visitations to his brain?

Outside their own front door stood the Christian Scientists. She looked more ashen than ever in her padded maroon robe, her husband as devoid of hope. I could easily understand why they'd been awakened. The screams, now joined by the crash of furniture, came from the apartment of Daniel and Alan, which was immediately below them.

But this was no time to commiserate with our huddled neighbors. Ignoring them, we bounded down numerous stairs at a time. The din grew louder with each step. With the thunder of large objects toppling mingled the tinkle of glass, shrill cries of protest — surely from Alan — punctuated by laughter that sometimes arched to a further scream.

By the time we reached their open door, Daniel was already a retreating figure in white silk pajamas heading downstairs and presumably to the front door of the building. There was already a wail of police sirens and, through the rain-distorted window above the foyer, the squat white shape of an ambulance.

But those outside activities dissolved before the bloody chaos confronting us in the apartment. The sounds from above had not lied: furniture had been upturned and flung at random, glass shards covered the floor, gore was everywhere. For a moment my heart stopped beating in fear that Eurydice's blood had created an abattoir of that living room and kitchen.

I shrieked at Ken to follow me into the bedroom. It, too, was empty — though there were gruesome stains, shiny wet on sopping sheets, an upturned chair, and a smashed side lamp. But the ceiling light was on, which enabled us to read the simple statement scrawled in lipstick across the length of a dressing-table mirror:

EURYDICE, I LOVE YOU!

We both stared at it, mesmerized by the blood red brilliance of the enormous letters and the stark plaint of the message. Then, in fine attune, we ran out of the place and down the remaining flight of stairs to where Daniel, his pajamas gruesomely stained, wrestled with a uniformed policeman and an ambulance attendant. A violently trembling Alan stood powerlessly watching his lover's assailants.

As we arrived, Daniel broke free. He pushed the ambulance man away with a violent shove, then immediately threw his arms around the officer and drew the surprised man's head toward his own. Just as the policeman recovered his poise and the attendant re-entered the fray, our demented poet threw back his head in the direction of a sobbing Alan.

"Eurydice," he screamed at the top of his voice, "Eurydice, may I kiss the cop?"

As they bundled him out into the rain, I thought I also heard him offer the cop a blow-job. If so, I never found out for sure. Daniel never returned to Century Apartments, and poor Eurydice dodged us after that horrible night. He too left very soon after. Ken said the manager of the building said that Alan couldn't afford the rent.

Anthony D. Miller — The stick kid

...Bright rent in this exquisite tapestry,

Glitter the eyes of a frightened faun
Who bites the red flowers with his small white teeth
Brown and bloody as the dregs of wine,
His lips part in laughter beneath a leaf
—Arthur Rimbaud

A stick kid: one you draw or erase, crumple up in a paper-wad basketball. All arms and legs, he stood, lean and shirtless, in tight jeans and stained sneakers. I cracked the screen door. His eyes were large, sleepy, wet, and brown. He made silence for me to break. Black hair fell in his right eye and over his shoulders. I shut the door in his face. The senior year in high school was underway. The summer before was over.

✳

I have been to the river since then. We leaned on the old tower bridge. You follow the pockmarked road — these days — that slopes from the old grade school. It just goes jagged and drops off where the bridge was. We held on to the sides. Sun beat down. When we shifted, our arms and elbows touched.

We were almost seventeen, Hat Trick and me. "Patrick Fitchett," his real name was. But I called him "Hat Trick" from the second day we met. When Beulah — the shaky-handed, pale homeroom teacher — called roll, she would say, "Jay Cullers?" and Hat Trick would yell, "Jay Bird!" She would get shakier and grayer. Hat Trick always called me that.

"You ever figure which one's the Massanutten and which one's the Blue Ridge?" he asked and lifted a beer bottle we'd stashed behind his radio.

"Hell if I know. Coach Shepard gave me a D in geography. I mean, all we did was take tests where you had to list the main crops in Hoodoo Land," I complained.

"Don't matter. You look downriver, it looks blue, like the river floats up over that mountain." He took the last swig. Foam ran down, streaking his tanned chest. He flipped the bottle upwards over the river. "Watch!"

The amber bottle rose and hung in midair. Sun penetrated and lit the glass. Falling took a long time. Spinning, it gave off sparks and flashes that exploded: a spray of embers on the rocks. "That's the way it is, Jay Bird."

The Shenandoah still makes its way around rocks, emits a smell of mud and fish, sounds as if voices gurgle up from the riverbed. You can stop short of the drop-off and cut through weeds. A wreckage of branches — gritty with silt — scatters the bank. You step over or walk along edges where mud spurts up your ankles. A brown water snake follows out of reach. Pointy head arching out of water, it gives you a quizzical look.

We sat on a fallen tree, a few yards down from where the new bridge was built. His radio sat between his feet — "So if it gets kicked over, you don't do it, Jay Bird." Hat Trick gave me drags off his Marlboros and told about spending nine months in Beaumont. Before his family moved to town, he broke into a little side-street grocery, down in Elton. "My dad and Shirley couldn't come see me

much. But, when they did, they'd bring stuff. You know —
chips, Zero bars, Cokes. I never got it though. Soon as
they'd leave, staff'd take it and say they had to check for
smokes or pocketknives. I'd never see it again."

Those branches the flood piled up, back in November,
have Johnny-jump-ups and bluebottles poking up at their
edges. A five o'clock shadow of weeds breaks out of mud
littered with brown-and-white mussel shells.

We jabbed at a black racer with our toes. He was all laid
out like a stick on the path. One poke and he coiled. I waved
a stick in front of that sucker. He struck and let out a hiss —
a sound like drawing breath in through your teeth. Hat
Trick tried getting him behind the head, but old racer was
too fast. That shiny black head was on and off his thumb
before Hat Trick knew what happened. He rinsed off blood.
We sat on the bank and split a cigarette. "What'd it feel
like?" I asked, eyeing the tooth marks.

"A real quick sting. Look at that motherfucker, still all
coiled and watching us."

"You don't figure it'll get infected?" I asked.

"Not likely. I heal pretty good. Like when I was first sent
to county jail, waiting for the sheriff to haul me down, I
resisted a little. They busted me up some. Never took me to
a doctor, anything. You know, boys would lay on those cots
and cry. I mean, cry loud. The deputies would yell, 'Stop,'
but those boys couldn't."

"Maybe Hat Trick?" I ventured.

"Yeah, I'll tell you that. Hell, Jay Bird, I tell you stuff.
Like back in the spring — that cold night — we went frog
gigging. We ended up rolling down the hill to the school,
just laughing. I never been that close with a dude before."
He stared at his sneakers.

"We're best friends, I guess." I crooked my arm over his
shoulder. Hat Trick met my gaze and grinned.

Then, his eyes went dry and cracked as winter ground.
"I told you I never got close to a dude. Well, now I have.

You leave me, Jay Bird, I'll hurt you." He stared into me.

"Sounds like a threat."

"I'm just saying, so you know."

The racer slipped toward a tree. He stopped now and then to stare at us. Like water running uphill, he climbed and tangled around a branch. When we came over to look, he drew his neck back — S-shaped — and flicked his tongue. I said, "I like that song." Hat Trick turned his radio up.

"Yeah, the Hollies — 'He Ain't Heavy, He's My Brother.' You like that, huh?"

Dutchman's breeches look more like little teeth hanging there. Turtles splatter off logs even if you walk up on them like an Indian. Out of the corner of your eye, you can catch fish darting in shallow water. Violets come close to outnumbering grass.

"One time, Jay Bird — did I tell you? — I was enjoying a good piss, and some big mother of a bumblebee came up out of nowhere. That thing just zoomed in a straight line, up after my pee. I panicked, for sure. Yanked my zipper. You want to talk pain!" Hat Trick said he felt free pissing outside. I said I didn't feel free much at all. "You take albums you don't like back. They believe you they're defective. Nobody checks, just for who your old man is."

"Don't start," I muttered.

"Your old lady doesn't want you hanging around me. I see it. We sit in your basement. She comes down those goddamned steps forty-six times. I mean, she offers me iced tea, cake, and stuff. But I see the way she looks at me."

"Okay. I get some shit. I don't need more from you." I turned my back on him and looked down.

"I don't believe you're for real, sometimes. Not yet." He spun me around and shoved me. We wrestled, laughed, and swore our heads off. Sprawled in mud, our clothes caked and our skin smeared, we laughed at each other's face. "Best friends?"

"Best friends," he answered. "You ever play chicken, Jay Bird?"

✳

"Salaama. Salaamon. Sooleimon." Neil Diamond on Hat Trick's radio. "Ta-ta-tum, ta-ta-tum" — three, maybe four times. I took the Marlboro in my lips. Hat Trick lit it. Diamond chanted, "Come, he come say. Ride on the night. Sun become day." We pressed our arms together, to the elbow, and put the cigarette where our arms met. "Day shall provide."

Those fine hairs burnt with an acrid smell. "Ta-ta-tum, ta-ta-tum. Soo-sooleimon. Soolei-soolei-sooleimon." Flesh burnt more acrid and went up my nose. Hat Trick's fist drew tighter, more clenched. "Soo-sooleimon. Soolei-soolei-sooleimon." His lip jutted. I clenched my teeth. Our arms tensed against each other. We dug our feet in at each other's toes. "Ta-ta-tum, ta-ta-tum, ta-ta-tum," frenzied.

"Great God of my want-want-want..." Touch a burner on high and stick fast. "Lord of my need-need-need..." Hat Trick's eyes were spinning, whirlpools, frisbees. The mud on his face and his lashes wet. "I can't fucking stand it." He spit. "Lean me on-on-on."

"We, we, we can stop." My voice broke. "Ta-ta-tum, ta-ta-tum, ta-ta-tum..."

"I can't," he whispered, tears changing mud on his face. "Bring home my name..." I tasted dirt and my tears. "On the wings of a flea..." Our feet twisted. "Wind in the plain..." Knees ground into one another. "Dance once for me..." Hat Trick twisted like he had to piss really bad. "Soo-sooleimon. Soolei-soolei-sooleimon..."

"Sweet Jesus. Sweet fucking Jesus!" I yelped.

"No-yeh-no-yeh-no-yeh!" he kept letting out like heart-beat, like breath. "Great God of my day-day-day. Lord of my night-night-night..." Our arms, I thought, melted to-gether. We pushed bone-deep. "Dance for the sun-sun-sun.

134

Seek for the way-way-way ... Take-a-me home..." Lunging backwards, he let the cigarette drop. Blackening some grass, it hissed and went out.

He laughed or cried, maybe both, with tears running and mud all over his face. Neither one of us got up from the grass and mud, spoke, or dropped eyes for some time. Eventually, he got up and sat in front of me. His forehead on mine, he rasped, "That's the way it is, Jay Bird." He took up my raw arm and blew on it.

✳

A copperhead draws under a rock and hides its penny-color face in thick coils. We never walked further than this. We might have ended up in Front Royal, where the river stinks of Avtex. Mama said Hat Trick was crazy. I didn't say I was at the time. Once, in the hall at school, he passed and slammed my shoulder hard with his. I said, "That took class," and he said, "Fuck you," without looking back.

I went on to college and learned everything I held inside was already put to words. Oscar Wilde: he said the world forgives its criminals, but not its dreamers.

Hat Trick knows I walk these unrequited places. Not on water, on edges. The mourning dove's call breaks and shatters. That's the way it is.

Guillermo Reyes Lorca's curse

Mrs. Capistrano sat across the table from her old friend Mrs. Lorca. She was counting her coins on the glass surface, one by one, sorting them out with her arthritic fingers into orderly piles. *"Un minutito, señora,"* she kept saying in a reassuring voice. "One little minute and we take care of this debt business, okay?"

Mrs. Lorca yawned. She squinted up at the southern California light that beamed down from the skylight and then burped. Maybe she doesn't care about the debt, thought Mrs. Capistrano, but she felt it was her duty as a debtor to pay back on time as agreed. She was prompt, she was reliable, she was a model debtor and proud of it. A few months previously, she'd broken her leg while working for a producer who never bought insurance for his maids. Mrs. Capistrano knew, however, that she could always rely on her old friend Mrs. Lorca, even if it hurt her deeply to borrow. More expenses lay ahead. Her leg hadn't healed and, when tested, was diagnosed with lupus. She didn't have long to live in fact, but she always paid her debts. On time. Soon enough, Mrs. Capistrano had piled a clump of coins on a stack of single dollar bills and slid them across the table. "There you go, señora," she said merrily. "Thirteen dollars and eighty-seven cents. Of course, I'll come next month to make another payment on the remaining $8,923.12 I now owe you. Yes?"

Mrs. Lorca shook her head, making her thirty-carat earrings swing like chili beans on her earlobes. "Don't be a peasant, Capistrano," she said in a typical mood. "Next month you might be dead. Me, too, for that matter. A quake could destroy Los Angeles any moment. You want more tea?" Mrs. Capistrano nodded as the heavyset Mrs. Lorca struggled to get up. Mrs. Capistrano reached out to help, but Mrs. Lorca looked annoyed. "You rest!" she ordered. "You're the one with the broken leg. I'm fat but not ill." Mrs. Capistrano looked away in shame. "You rest and don't say a word." Mrs. Lorca slowly made her way through the room until she disappeared through a door that led to the kitchen.

Mrs. Capistrano let out a sigh of relief. She was finally alone in the grand, airy room of the Lorca mansion. She reached for her cane and decided to make a quick excursion through the room, searching for valuables that might fit inside her purse. Mrs. Capistrano was not a thief, but she was a certified kleptomaniac. Mrs. Lorca knew this, but was too rich to care.

Ah, yes, the Lorcas, thought Mrs. Capistrano. The Lorcas had come far in this world. Perhaps too far for common Mexicans like herself, thought Mrs. Capistrano, not without resentment. But of course none of this success could be attributed to Mrs. Lorca's talents. Her son, Little Tony, Toñito, now known to the world as Anthony Lorca, had come up with a marketable product: his chest. Tony had done well on film without his shirt. The life-sized pictures of him hanging in the hallways of the mansion told the story in vivid, alluring colors. The boy had been cast in the right roles as a sort of "ethnic honcho." In his latest film,

Tony would invade Grenada and liberate his kidnapped girlfriend, who was being held as a sexual slave by communist terrorists supported by a liberal congress. He'd also be required to make R-rated love to the various starlets in the film.

Recently, however, a controversy had arisen when some of the actresses refused to kiss Tony on the lips for fear of contracting AIDS. Much gossip and speculation went around, and the issue had not yet been settled. That day, Mrs. Capistrano kept her ears open for any recent developments on the issue, but so far not a word from Mrs. Lorca.

Meanwhile, Mrs. Capistrano had her eye on a lovely crystal vase. Her pawnbroker adored crystal, and she herself was lured by its sparkling beauty. But there was no way to fit it into her purse, and by then Mrs. Lorca could be heard approaching with a tray.

"Tea time again!" Mrs. Lorca chimed joyously, sounding really stupid. The hostess placed the tray down and went through the entire ritual of asking how many lumps of sugar Mrs. Capistrano would take with her tea, cream or no cream, butter or no butter on the pastries. "The maid buys them for me on Santa Monica Boulevard," she said. "You know which part of Santa Monica Boulevard?" she asked. Mrs. Capistrano shrugged without an idea. "Come on, guess!" she insisted. "Don't be stupid. Which part? Well, the part where all the *homos* hang out," she finally explained, emitting a hoarse little giggle.

Mrs. Capistrano looked away, embarrassed, clutching protectively at her teacup. Mrs. Lorca and her vulgar expressions, she thought. Some things never changed. When the two had met some twenty years ago, they'd known each other vaguely as "that other Mexican servant across the street." One day, Mrs. Lorca had shown up on her day off with Corona beer and unfiltered cigarettes in hand. After some months, she started showing up with sailors, one for each of the women. Back then, the last thing they would have cared about was drinking tea. Yes, that one detail of consumption had changed, but Mrs. Lorca's way of talking, her basic expressions, had remained intact.

"So is everything all right, my friend?" asked Mrs. Capistrano. "You seem a little happier today, serving me tea and everything."

Mrs. Lorca aimed a sugar cube from a distance. It landed inside of Mrs. Capistrano's cup, and she giggled in delight.

"What? Me? Happy?" she laughed. "I'm just getting older, how about you?" Before Mrs. Capistrano could answer, she went on. "How are your boys? Will they get out of jail soon? It's about time, you know." She was holding out the pastries on a platter, her arm shaking with a beginning case of Parkinson's. The bloodhounds were sniffing their way through the room, nibbling at the pastries and then, not satisfied, inspecting Mrs. Capistrano's bandaged leg. "*Ya vayanse!*" Mrs. Lorca was stomping her fat foot on the wooden floor.

Mrs. Capistrano was feeling dizzy, put on edge by the dogs, which she feared, made nervous by Mrs. Lorca's strange questions. She felt an urge to run out, to breathe fresh air.

Before she could answer Mrs. Lorca, Tony Lorca walked in, dressed in a long, satin bathrobe. He was followed by two shirtless young men with stiffly moussed hair, dressed in polka-dot shorts. Each carried pads and pencils, taking notes as Tony spoke.

"No, no, no!" exclaimed Tony. "We are not going to let the publicity go unanswered!" Mrs. Lorca turned to offer some tea, but he was already serving himself. He nodded at Mrs. Capistrano, faintly acknowledging her presence. "You call this tea, Mami?" he asked, spitting it out into the cup. "It doesn't have that Ceylon zap I've come to expect after years of travel!"

"Oh, after ten cups who cares?" exclaimed Mrs. Lorca, who was on her eleventh cup of the day.

"Who has time to drink more than one at a time?" he asked, forbidding the secretaries to sit and serve themselves. He turned to Mrs. Lorca. "We have an emergency, Mother, and you're going to do your share."

One of the secretaries, a young man with stiff nipples, interrupted diplomatically. "Mrs. Lorca has already expressed her unwillingness to cooperate."

"Nonsense, surfer boy!" retorted Tony, squeezing his tit. "The reporter from *People* magazine will be here any minute, and Mami here will give him the family angle we need. *Good Housekeeping* follows later, and maybe the *Saturday Evening Post* as well."

Mrs. Lorca crossed her fat legs, looking stubborn. "I don't give interviews," she said.

"Oh, really?" said Tony, smiling. "You're not important enough to refuse interviews, Mami. Sorry. We need the mother angle now that those bitches have refused to kiss me on the set."

"But, Mr. Lorca," the hairy-chested second secretary said, "we could always use a substitute mother."

"A what?"

"An actress willing to play the role of Mrs. Lorca."

"I am not a fake!" Tony protested, insulted. The secretary grew quiet and submissive, but he was used to it. "Now I need time to think, think, think. I got it!" he said, turning to the secretaries, who looked up in expectation. "We'll take a swim and then worry about it later." Before long, the men had stripped to red swimsuits and were running out to the pool.

"Queers," Mrs. Lorca muttered out loud, and Mrs. Capistrano looked away, pretending she hadn't heard. Mrs. Lorca turned to the quiet little woman. "Anyway, Capistrano, you never told me how your boys are doing in prison."

"Fine," said Mrs. Capistrano faintly. "Just fine."

"I'm bored!" announced Mrs. Lorca. "I guess we'll just have to look at the family jewels again."

"No, we don't have to," begged Mrs. Capistrano, beginning to feel the sweat of kleptomania on the tips of her fingers.

"But I want to," said Mrs. Lorca. She pulled out a shimmering collection of diamonds and emeralds from a safe behind a picture of Lorca's muscular chest, which was bulkier than any woman's. "Tony always comes with me to Rodeo Drive to help me select the finest jewels." Mrs. Lorca held a diamond up to the light and slowly brought it down, nearly touching Mrs. Capistrano's mouth. "Wouldn't you like to swallow one?" she asked.

"*Que, señora?*" Mrs. Capistrano felt her dentures wiggle in her mouth.

"It's what thieves do, right? They swallow jewels. It's what you've been thinking all along, isn't it?" Mrs. Lorca picked out one of her least favorites. "Swallow this one. I don't like the cut. But I'm sure you'll have fun digging for it in your toilet bowl afterwards."

Mrs. Capistrano felt her body rise like a disturbed spirit from her chair. "I should go now."

"Sit down, Capistrano!" Mrs. Lorca's hand pressed into the bones of the little woman's shoulder. "It's your family curse, isn't it?"

"What curse?"

"Everybody's got one. Your kids are common criminals, petty thieves. They're in jail for a reason, aren't they?"

"Well, they may be thieves, but at least they're not..." Mrs. Capistrano stopped, realizing she'd fallen into Mrs. Lorca's trap.

"Say it, your boys are not what? Say it, Capistrano, and then I'll let you swallow this one with your tea. I know what you're thinking, Capistrano. You were supposed to be my friend, but you're just like the rest, believing the rumors about my Tony. Well, the rumors are true! So there! And it's only because of the family curse."

Before she could elaborate, Tony and the boys had come running in, dripping all over the floor, and had rushed upstairs. "The reporters will be here any minute," complained Tony at the secretaries, "and you creatures are running around half-naked." He turned to his mother. "And it's a major crisis when that maid takes her day off and you have to lick these secretaries' boots to get them to do some cooking!"

Mrs. Capistrano hadn't dared move. Mrs. Lorca, more quietly, more subdued, sat beside her. "If you must know, Capistrano, there are perfectly good reasons for the boy's condition. Sooner or later, I had to tell you all about ... the curse."

Mrs. Capistrano looked skeptical. "I guess I don't really believe in curses."

"Shut up. Let me explain. From the top..."

Mrs. Lorca reviewed the basics of her own humble upbringing in an impoverished neighborhood in Guadalajara, Mexico. During the evenings, young people would find little to do except sit around with adults listening to soap operas on the radio. She was special. She preferred to loiter on the streets with young, manly men. "Real men," she called them. "They were my favorite." She sat by the sidewalks, three or four popular young men around her, some of them soccer players, or soldiers on leave, or seminary students unsure of their vocation. They would tell dirty jokes; pass around sticks of gum, cigarettes, beer; feel her legs; and hurl insults at passersby. One of the people her crowd enjoyed tormenting was the local *"maricón."* But it was his fault, she claimed. He made no effort to hide his condition, and even nuns would often lecture him on overcoming his fanciful way of walking. He was defiant. He would often drop his handkerchief in front of the brutal boys, hoping one of them would pick it up and take him home with him.

"The audacity," cried Mrs. Lorca, "the audacity of that *maricón* to feel no shame, and then to end up crying when we expressed what was in our hearts about him. After a few punches, he'd run away, but turn around and blow kisses our way with his face all bloody. He just never gave up. So finally the boys couldn't stand his abuse any longer and beat the *mierda* out of him. I helped. I stole his purse and used the mascara and lipstick on my next date — when I got pregnant."

"What about the police?" Mrs. Capistrano stuffed her face with a third scone, nearly choking when she spoke up. "Didn't somebody call the police when all this violence occurred?"

"Of course!" Mrs. Lorca smiled proudly. "The police came and took the *maricón* away."

The man got a couple of months in jail for disturbing the peace and for blowing kisses at the other men. When released from jail, he moved away with a couple of old aunts to another neighborhood, where things didn't turn out much different. "Standards of decency are the same throughout Mexico," she added boastfully. "Heck, throughout Latin America."

She went on with her story. Months had gone by. Her pregnancy had started to show, but none of the men with whom she'd been acquainted offered to take responsibility for her child. "So for months on end I dragged this load around like a rock with no one's help," she said, not bothering to clarify the touchy matter of the father's identity. "My parents thought I was a *puta* and threw me out ... I lived on and off with friends and relatives before I came to the U.S."

On the night before her departure to Los Angeles, she was walking home after a triple feature of Esther Williams films. She took a badly lit alley, where she'd usually bum cigarettes from the sailors. No one was around on that cold winter night. As she walked, she realized she was being followed. She tried to pick up her pace, but the load slowed her down. She quickly ran out of breath and decided to stop and confront her pursuer. She turned and, to her horror, found that it was *him*.

"It was the *maricón!*" she exclaimed as Mrs. Capistrano held on to the edge of her seat. "Scars crisscrossed his face as if he'd been injured so many times there was no place left on it for anyone to hurt him. I thought he'd beat me and rape me, but, as you know, that was impossible — he was a *maricón!* So I was brave and I faced him. 'What do you want, *chica?*' I asked. You had to get tough with him, you see."

In the moonlight, she saw his fierce, glimmering eyes done in heavy makeup, beaming a strange glare at her. At first, it seemed malicious, but when he spoke up, his face suddenly radiated sympathy and benevolence. She wasn't sure what to think. There he was, the *maricón*, telling her all of a sudden she could come live with him, that he'd heard of her troubles with her family, that the neighborhood practically thought she was a slut, that they could settle across town and start a business of a reputable kind. Nobody would know much about them, they could start anew. "Imagine the audacity!" she cried. "He wanted me to live with him!" He insisted. She started to walk away. He followed. She threatened to call the police. "I told him I would raise my son by myself in a decent household, that if I wanted to give my child a father, it sure wouldn't be a *maricón!*" His face grew rigid, harsh. She felt endangered.

"In that case," the man had said, speaking in a matter-of-fact tone of voice, "if your child is a boy, I will make sure the Virgin of Guadalupe turns him into one of *us*. Your boy will be blessed. To you, it'll be a curse; to us, a dream come true." He was laughing, and she was feeling frail and dizzy. She finally swooned, falling to the pavement, reaching up to the sky thinking she could cling to fragmented lights there. When she came to she was being led into the maternity ward, where she gave birth to her boy.

"And that's how Tony Lorca became one of *them*," Mrs. Lorca said, sipping her tea. "I told you there's an explanation for everything, Capistrano. Capistrano?"

Mrs. Capistrano had devoured all the crumpets on the plate as if she'd been gobbling down cheap popcorn at a rundown movie theater. "That's quite a story, *que no?*" she finally commented, forcing a grin. She'd already decided that the next time a payment was due she would send a money order through the mail. "A curse, huh?"

"I told myself one day I'd break the curse. I tried being tough, using corrective measures like blows in the head with a stick, to toughen him, strengthen him, you know. But here we are instead," she said, spreading her arms to exhibit her mansion. "Cash is my compensation, I guess."

Cash is not just a compensation, thought Mrs. Capistrano, but a blessing, one that she would have exchanged for grandchildren anytime. And to think the Lord had blessed her with two perfectly normal boys whose lust for life had inspired them to burglarize a few Beverly Hills homes. She did not necessarily approve of their actions, but judging by the various illegitimate children they had left behind, her sons had proved to be as manly as the characters played by Tony Lorca on film.

"Come on, say something!" Mrs. Lorca nudged Mrs. Capistrano, who seemed entranced in prayer. Mrs. Lorca looked eager for feedback. "You have heard about the scandal, right? You know what he was talking about."

"Oh, no, no." Mrs. Capistrano thought it best to deny everything. "I don't keep up with Hollywood gossip."

"But that's it, don't you see?" Mrs. Lorca's eyes gleamed in expectation. "The Hollywood gossip will break the curse. Maybe all is lost — the reputation, the cash, the glamor — and we are free, and he has to go to work and find a woman to support. Hollywood will break the curse!"

At that moment, Tony Lorca walked in. He wore a luminous suit, beige, with lapels and broad shoulders. A curse or a blessing, Mrs. Capistrano kept thinking. Was he a curse or a blessing? "The reporters have arrived, and I have served them caviar and champagne by the pool. I suppose I could always make a living as a waiter again if everything else falls to pieces. So it's your turn, Mami. They want to hear the story of your life — hopefully, the censored version." Mrs. Lorca wouldn't budge. "Come on, we need the family-oriented publicity."

He gave a studied look at both the women and arrived at a quick conclusion. "You haven't been talking about that curse again, have you? What an embarrassment! And you wonder how these rumors get started! In my own home, no less. Now, come on, you're going to talk to that reporter!"

An argument ensued between mother and son. Mrs. Lorca insisted that fate had come calling. The curse would at last be broken, she claimed. Both poverty and happiness lay ahead.

There was no sign of shock or surprise in Tony Lorca's expression. Mrs. Capistrano watched him walk out and quickly return with new proof sheets of the publicity pictures for his next film, *The Patriot's Revenge*, showing Tony Lorca in macho poses. Picture by picture, one could see Mrs. Lorca's face lighten in the illusive hope of seeing her son on the silver screen yet again, as America's toughest, nastiest, roughest. She was swept away by the illusion, by the feeling that all again was fine with her life, with her world, with her adopted country itself. It didn't take much to convince her that she was in fact the mother of the most masculine man in America.

Mrs. Lorca was up now, her weight apparently less bulky and a lot more manageable. She pulled the makeup kit from her purse and plastered her face with creams and powder. Mrs. Capistrano could see the change, could even believe that this woman was now leaner, prettier, somehow glamorous. Son and mother exited, arm in arm, leaving the guest to wonder in awe.

But more importantly, Mrs. Capistrano was now alone with the case of jewels. There they were, sparkling at her, bewitching and seductive. Only one, she told herself. She could probably get away with taking one. She lifted one of the diamonds into her mouth, nervously, looking around to make sure nobody was watching. She picked up her cup of tea with her other hand, and she drank the tea and the jewel together. She felt it rolling down her throat like an aphrodisiac.

But the feeling, the hunger, wasn't satisfied. She wanted and desperately yearned for another one. She repeated the action, found the second one rough on her throat, scratching it. But it didn't matter. She was out of control. She swallowed a third, then a fourth, then a fifth. She had finally taken eight with her tea, like precious crumpets. Her stomach was no longer churning.

She felt the urge to run now, but couldn't. Her leg dragged behind her. She headed for the door. About a hundred yards were left before reaching the gate and, with it, freedom. But before she could reach it, she found her path obstructed by the bloodhounds, their eyes glaring at her, their snouts drooling.

"Now, come on, Judy and Mickey," she said. Mrs. Lorca had named the dogs after the grandchildren she wished she might have had. "*Sean buenitos* — you relax and let me out, yes?"

Instead, she heard the dogs' feet unbolt from the ground like the charge of cavalry. At this point, she saw in the polluted sky the luminous figure of the Virgin of Guadalupe, bedecked in expensive, glittery robes, holding her naked child. She expected a hand to reach out and lift her to the heavens. Instead, the Virgin's eyes shone back at her with dollar bills in their sockets, and her halo gave off the glow of gold. The beasts' fangs bit deep into the cancerous bone of her leg. She screamed, fell, and looked up. The Virgin still stood there, her boy playfully messing up her hair with his fingers. But her eye sockets were empty and blood trickled from them like red tears. *"Putamadre!"* she screamed angrily at her in a deep howl before she fell and died.

Ron Woewoda Still the night

"Cleanse the mind," the Buddhadhasa has said, "and the body will likewise become clean."

Here in the monastery I have spent much time attempting to achieve the cleansing state of calm. Indeed, I do attain it daily, and at these times I feel assured of my success.

The days are spent simply. We forty men are awakened at five. Meditation, yoga, breathing exercises, and two small meals — this is our day. The lanterns are doused at ten. I know the routine instinctively now — it is lodged in every cell of my body. I move from dormitory to kitchen hut to meditation field without conscious thought. I eat and I drink without tasting. I sit and I walk without seeing.

But the nights! The nights explode into Technicolor flashes of pornography and threatened violence. My mind sweeps the cutting-room floor of my past, selects scenes, then exaggerates and embellishes, enhances and expands.

"With time the past will cease to be and the future will lose its urgency," says the Attained One. "You will live solely in the beauty of the present. Even in sleep the tranquility will spread and blossom to encompass the entire being."

I have been adhering to a vow of silence — a catalyst, He has said — toward the achievement of perfect calm.

Minutes after the lanterns have been extinguished, the gabble begins — seventeen hours of silence collapse into raucous laughter and strident voices in the dark.

How do I silence these voices? Do I want to?

✳

My doctor did it well that morning, I'll give her that. She put on her best, most comforting smile before she destroyed me.

That smile. From childhood measles and mumps through teenage attacks of acne and insecurity, it had given me faith in her healing powers. With the aid of pills and potions she could kiss the hurt and make it better. This new smile bespoke only helpless compassion.

She stood. Arrogant sunlight shone through the window behind her, skittered off the stainless steel and enamel. She came around the desk and perched on its corner — close enough to comfort but not to heal.

"I'll be honest with you," she said. This alerted me, said that perhaps she wasn't always. It told me that her omnipotence had vanished.

"I don't know that much about it yet," she continued, "But come on, we'll get through it. It doesn't have to mean the end."

Bullshit. That's exactly what it meant. She knew it. I knew it.

The virus had destroyed her power. Now it was poised and waiting to destroy me.

She squeezed my shoulder, squeezed tears from my eyes, sobs from my throat.

✳

...Cairo, the bus terminus where I met him the first time. I know he will show, but I continually consult my wristwatch to assure myself that I have not been waiting long. The blue exhaust from the buses hangs on the hot, foul, August air. The platform of cracked, buckling concrete is crowded, and I am jostled and pushed as the rattling, stinking buses arrive and depart.

A man in a light cotton galabiya is leaning against a steel pole. He has a hand in his pocket and periodically displays what it holds. He has an erection, and I find it impossible to avoid looking. Each time I do he leers and tosses his head, indicating that I should walk in that direction. If I do, he will follow. I want to, but the other should be here soon.

Five minutes, I decide, and check my watch once more.

The man has moved and is now standing behind me in the crowd. He steps forward a little and cranes as though searching for the number of his bus. As he does, he rubs against me. I can feel his breath on my neck; it is hot and garlicky, and there is excitement in it. I lean backward and press into his body. As I do, I spot the one I have been waiting for. I hesitate, press a moment longer, then without turning I move through the crowd...

✳

How long has it been? Months, certainly. Two? Three?

Here, time is purported to be of little significance, yet this morning it is my first question as the monk strikes the conical bell outside the dormitory.

(the dream-men are there still, fluttering like dark moths, just outside my vision)

I rise and make my way along the dark path to the bathing cistern.

I remove my sarong and pour dippers of cold water over my head. Shock rivers down my back and chest. All around me male bodies are doing the same. Naked male bodies, but they hold no interest — the calm has resettled, and I am oblivious to their presence.

151

We forty move as one from the dormitory to the meditation field. My identity blurs into the mass as we silently
parade through the dark woods which separate the living
area from the field.

The field activates switches. They trigger the flow of
tranquility and unleash the waves of serenity. I assume
Lotus position on the reed mat, and the first ripples begin
to wash over me.

"Clear the mind," we were told. For the thousandth
time I do.

"Concentrate on the breath." I do.

Slowly the ripples are replaced by waves of calm and
weightlessness.

✳

More tests and her knowledge of the virus is increased.
Some of this she shares. She administers the pieces carefully for they are equipped with time-release. They are in-
gested slowly and at first seem logical, palatable even.
Days, weeks later, they come to full power, and what they
release is terror.

In one of her regurgitations she informs me that the virus
can eventually pollute the brain. This not only compounds
my fear but causes me to begin doubting my sanity. She
assures me that if it begins to happen she will know, but I am
aware that my mind is not her greatest concern. Her sermons tell me to change jobs, quit smoking, calm down.

"You can have some control in this, you know. Two,
three years, maybe more if you do it right."

I cannot accept these limits, and I ignore her demands.

"Stress," she says, "will only speed up the process. Your
weakness is its strength. It feeds on it."

She is right. My body begins to mutiny. Rashes appear,
stay a week, vanish. My gums inflame, bleed, heal only to
inflame and bleed the next week or the week after.

I live in constant vigilance against the next manifestation. Every pimple becomes suspect, every sniffle a sure sign.

She sees these changes, and the sermons become pleas.

✳

...Mombasa, and I am sitting on a pile of timbers watching the dhows in the harbor being loaded. Men, broad and black, are shouldering massive burlap sacks and running down the inclined planks that cross the muddy, green water between the dock and the ships. The scene conjures images formed by childhood stories: galleons loaded with gold bullion and spice, pirate ships flying the skull and crossbones.

A tall, black man in a khaki uniform walks toward me. He stops, rests a leather boot on the timber, surveys me from behind dark glasses.

"What are you doing here?" he asks.

"Just looking," I say defensively.

"This is a restricted area. Show me your passport."

Jee-zuz, I think, here we go.

"I don't have it," I say, "It's at the hotel. I was walking in the market and didn't want to carry it with me."

"Come. You must follow me."

He leads me to a cinder-block cube which is an office between the warehouses.

Inside it is dim and cool. A ceiling fan whirs, shifting the air in chunks. The frosted jalousie windows are closed, muzzling the din of the harbor.

"Sit," he says, pointing to a bench against one wall. He crosses to the door, flips the dead bolt.

"What the..." But he is on me; his mouth on mine, thick-lipped and rough. I try pushing him away, but he has me wedged against the wall. He outweighs me by a hundred pounds.

His ham-hand kneads, pushes clothing, his fingers dig painfully.

He stands, pulls open his belt, yanks at his trousers. He gestures toward me, demands: "Take them off."

He peels off his shirt and steps out of his trousers.

He smells of burnt cinnamon and musk.

He pulls me, smothers me in huge arms and darkness...

✳

The brass bowl is lightly tapped with an iron striker. The metallic reverberations signify the end of the morning meditation.

It was not a good session for me. Several novices arrived yesterday, and they are not yet accustomed to sitting stationary for two hours. They wriggle and shift, they cough and sniffle. I allowed their agitation to distract my concentration, and I did not reach my usual depth of calm.

Though perhaps the blame is misplaced. I am troubled by the dreams and fear that they may be sabotaging my efforts.

(...the brain-pollution may assist here — it may come to short-circuit this nocturnal flow of passion...)

I rise from the mat in the shade of the tree and slowly walk toward the trail which leads to the kitchen hut.

We all move slowly here. When I first arrived, I was uneasy at the zombie movements. I know now that it is the absence of impatience, a conquering of the habit of projecting oneself into an expected future situation.

"You cannot speed the sunrise," says Buddhadhasa, and I have learned to quell my anticipation. The calm grows.

✳

"Try it. That's all I'm asking. Try it," she says. An extended finger taps staccato on the cover of the medical journal lying on her desk.

154

We have been waging a tug-of-war for most of the morning.

"It can work," she says emphatically and sits back waiting for me to confirm that she has won.

The journal contains her latest ammunition: case studies of death being cheated, documentation of faceless marvels achieving remission after time in solitude and quiet. I am skeptical and have accused her of witchcraft and grasping at straws, but I admit that I have to do something. I cannot just wait. The sores have become a soft, rotten purple. The fears are exploding into panic.

"Yeah, okay, let's do it."

She smiles. Some of her old power has returned.

※

...Istanbul. February and the winter is still heavily upon the city. Wood-carriers with their backs bent under bundles of sticks labor up and down the cobbled hills — a city of two million is heated by wood fires. The smoke mixes with the fog and the misty drizzle to paint a grimy patina onto the red brick and the limestone of the buildings.

I stop at a cinema and climb the short flight of stairs to the sheltered entrance. I look at posters of adventure films. A young man is standing alone in the corner near the doors of the theatre. I realize that he has been watching me, and I smirk in his direction as I light a cigarette. He maintains his level gaze and smiles. With a heave of his shoulder he pushes away from the wall and moves toward me.

He opens rapid-fire babble. I shake my head.

"English?" I ask.

He wags his head of black hair. No, no English.

His eyes are soft and amber-colored. They contain invitation, and I follow as he descends the stairway into the street.

As we walk his arm sways, brushes against my leg. I am excited by this and hope that wherever he is leading us is not far. We walk many blocks and leave the center of the city. Office buildings and shops give way to narrow two-story houses and frozen scrubby vegetable plots with goats tethered in corners. He points across a small field to a hill, and I nod assent.

There is a dilapidated shed. It smells of rotting wood and dampness. Entering it I am nervous and suddenly aware that I know nothing about him.

It is warmer out of the wind, and we remove our gloves and open our jackets. Black hairs escape over the top of his shirt, and I notice for the first time how poorly dressed he is.

His hand floats to the nape of my neck. Our mouths meet, and I am surprised by the sweetness of his tongue. I expect something more crude, a peasant flavor to match his clothes.

He steps away. We remove our coats and open our shirts.

His skin is scalding against mine after the cold of the air, and we press hard against each other.

I feel him tense and press even closer.

We hold on long after the waves recede.

Warm.

Close.

As wax, I am melting, flowing into him. Into his safe warmth...

❋

It is very warm in the field this afternoon. The air is motionless and filled with the smell of scorching grass and drying trees. There is a constant electric buzz of insect noise which is interrupted only by the occasional squawk or trill of birds.

But I am soon unaware of any of this. The smells and the heat and the sounds quickly retreat to somewhere vaguely distant.

Follow the breath from the point of entry.

Follow it into the lungs.

Follow its exit.

The novices have been excused because of the temperature, and there is no distraction. The switches are thrown, and the calm arrives.

I ride on undulating currents of placid control. There is no tension, there is nothing ... only calm.

✳

At these times, in the quiet euphoria which lingers in the echoing of the brass, after hours of riding the waves of a pervading peace, fear is an alien intruder. It is something foreign, and I can view it dispassionately as though from a distance. This sensation of detachment allows me to examine the virus without the revolted horror which before flooded my mind at its first thought. Then it was as a dead rat which I held by the tail. My mind would fling the thought away in anger and revulsion.

✳

...Gran Canaria and a midnight beach. Wind carries sea salt over the dunes, and the air is sweet-sour. A stranger is following me, yet he wanders at a distance which will make our meeting seem as coincidence. I stop, and he comes closer. Our eyes lock, and there is agreement. There is also familiarity and something which does not belong — a sensation of emotional *déjà vu*.

He lives nearby, he says, and we again begin walking.

It is a small bungalow. He plays Chopin on the stereo and gives me wine while he fills the tub with steaming water and bubbling soap.

I ease myself awkwardly into the water to face him.

He has lit the room with a candle. This seems contrived to me. I seek out his eyes in the gloom to reassure myself. They are black and deep and hold no flicker of the insincerity I suspect — he is reading me too. This brief inspection satisfies something in us both, and our fingers mesh in the water. Eyes maintain contact and the recognition which began on the beach now grows into a haunting but comforting certainty.

I slide down the porcelain and curl my legs behind his back. We lean forward and embrace. This is uncomfortable, but it seems important to prolong it.

The water becomes lukewarm. We fondle with thin towels and move to the bed. Eyes find eyes and fingers reach. Light as flies, they land on cheeks, brows, chins.

It is surreality swirling in slow motion. Lust is buried, concealed beneath the enormity of what we are sharing.

He rests a leg on mine. This new warmth is magnetic and pulls me to him. Yet eyes remain fixed, seeing deeper, deeper.

Hands move to faces. Each holds the other's head as a precious object, something of awe.

Then his fingers press harder against my temples. His head stiffens and enlarges in my palms as his jaws clench and his black eyes become wild and laughing.

Then I fall. I fall into those eyes which are now calmer but filled with tears. And I sob too as the surges ebb to ripples, subside to calm.

※

I awake before the monk strikes the bell. I awake to a void. I realize — at first in a moment of panic — that I have no recollection of the night. Then the calm comes.

The bell is struck.

Slowly I move to the cistern. Slowly I join the other men and move to the field.

Slowly ... slowly...

Thomas Losito
I am here now I am gone

Light shattered upon the movement of the water; the waves spewed rainbows as they burst upon the shore. Terence raised his hand to shield his eyes from the glare. A statue, a naked Adonis, carved of the most sublime alabaster, stood waist-deep in the water and, turning, walked slowly toward the shore. Terence continued walking, and as they passed they smiled in recognition of each other. Curled ends of blond hair holding drops of water like jewels framed the Adonis's face. They spoke with each other while sitting on the sandy part of the beach, and when his companion decided to go back for another swim, Terence removed his shorts and followed. Is it love, Terence wondered, when you hold a beautiful face, kissing it softly, eyelashes brushing each other's cheeks, eyes glinting like the flashing of a crystal turning slowly on a string; when you embrace and the world melts and sounds are sucked into silence and not one thought ruffles the glassy smoothness of perfect pleasure? In an hour, in less than an hour, this stranger will vanish from my life forever, Terence thought. One more look, one more touch. As they embraced a part of him knew that familiarity was the killer; time together would erode the absoluteness of the moment and make of their passion something ordinary, predictable. The very pain of letting go (acutely aware of each second as his fingers slipped along a silken shoulder), this moment plunged in the crucible, purifying his desire, made of it something resilient, smooth, brilliant with a light that brings tears, a consuming and indestructible thing.

Terence pulled on his shorts, and as he stepped carefully over the rocks toward the sandy part of the beach, he paused. Among the scattered stones lay a stone in the perfect shape of a heart. He picked it up and turned it between his fingers as if contemplating a piece of a puzzle. A sign, he thought, smiling at the irony of it. He flung it into the waves.

Later, at the party in Truro, sitting alone by a window, he remembered almost nothing they had said to each other, but every detail of their lovemaking... (what was his name — David, yes, like the statue). He sighed as the experience formed itself into another memory; another ring forming in the pool of his emotions where he had dropped a stone, where his passion had risen up for a moment, and now swept outward and away, a fading ripple. Light sifted through the darkness as the fog came steaming off the ocean. He thought for a moment that he saw a figure with glistening skin forming in the folds of the mist.

Paul hesitated, watching Terence intently before engaging him in conversation. Something about Terence had evoked a memory of Drew from the previous summer. It seemed a lifetime ago to Paul. It was Terence's profile, the sadness in his eyes, the stillness of his reverie; and when he shifted his head slightly, all at once Paul saw Drew and remembered how he had loved him most in those moments of repose.

He was lying beside him — the paper shades lit by the moon became a row of ghosts, witnessing.

160

"We have to end it," Drew had said, softly. "I think Robert knows."

Moonlight lay like iron over the bed, weighing Paul down.

"I think I have it," the words floated out of Drew, disembodied, surreal, a ripple passing over the silence which the room held tentatively, like a cracked bowl.

Paul held him then, not knowing why. Perhaps because the words had frozen his heart and he needed warmth, any warmth. Is it because of Robert, he had thought — he would not, could not speak — or because you have it? Pale light seeped through the cracks slowly filling the room. The words were the light, illuminating imperfectly, without color, becoming the emptiness that spread though him.

Thereafter he could not tolerate moonlight, or even twilight; and those days when the sun became a pale gray disk floating behind clouds filled him with despair. Only in the brilliance of a seamless blue sky or in the embrace of a starless black night did he feel that his life was not disintegrating. Half-light, like half-truth, had become intolerable to him.

Paul trembled slightly. As he began the conversation with Terence, he explained his nervous disorder, describing it as one of the symptoms of the AIDS virus. While they spoke Terence found himself thinking about a close friend who had died of AIDS the summer before. The memory of that time echoed through a dark gulf, reverberating, bringing other memories with it. The experience had changed him, or rather, it had exposed a deeper level of his personality which had been buried all his life. It was himself which he saw now, and yet it was someone else, someone who filled him with fear. Sometimes he saw him in a stranger's face in a bar, or heard him in the voice of a friend who was taking AZT, or felt him lying heavily by his side on a sleepless night; and, more and more, saw him in dreams. He felt cut off from his past, his youth, and when he looked toward his future, he could see only the shadows of losses obscuring his path.

"Robert and I rent this cottage every year for a month," said Paul. "We decided to start this season with a party — just close friends. With my condition we're not sure how much time is left."

Terence admired Paul's candor. He remembered how his friend, usually so reserved, had become very outspoken in direct proportion to the disease's progress. Paul evoked memories of a life Terence felt he had lived a hundred years ago.

"So, you came with Mark," said Paul.

"Yes, we spent this week at a guest house in Provincetown. Actually we had planned to come up two weeks ago, but when Mark got the invitation to the party, and since Truro's so close, we decided to come up this week instead."

"Are you and Mark involved?" Paul asked, nonchalantly.

"No! We're just friends," exclaimed Terence, laughing.

Paul smiled, obviously satisfied with the response.

"You're too much," said Terence, shaking his head.

Robert was watching Paul and Terence furtively, while mingling with the other guests, slowly working his way toward them. Paul was asking Terence other personal questions, and not to be outdone, Terence was making up outrageous responses. They laughed together like conspirators. Without interrupting Robert pulled up a chair. He heard two conversations simultaneously; that between Paul and Terence, and an interior and ubiquitous dialogue of pain. Gradually the voices dimmed, the friends and lover, the room, the cottage, disintegrated as the ocean in the distance began to flow toward him. He visualized a sand castle melting as the waves lapped like hungry tongues. The way of escape had been cut off by the water as the sand castle became an island growing smaller and smaller. Sadness filled him as another wave broke at his feet. He stared at the sand where the retreating waves had exposed bare, smooth skin, and etched a face. He was back in the cottage, in the room, staring at Terence, who was sitting next to him and opposite Paul, forming the base of a triangle.

Terence kept glancing at Robert. He began to feel the smooth blade of desire brushing lightly over his skin; and when Robert spoke — a beautiful voice, sensual and lilting — the blade turned and pierced him. Unconsciously he turned his wineglass by the fluted stem, slowly, the movement lulling him into a reverie as he imagined his hands like combs, slipping through Robert's long, black hair — he could feel the silkiness of it — and his fingertips lightly touching the pale temples.

"Why don't you stay?" Paul was asking.

Terence blinked. The spell was broken.

"I'm sorry, what did you say?"

"Why don't you stay with us for a couple of weeks. The sofa opens into a bed."

"Well, I —" he hesitated, taken aback by the abruptness of the invitation.

"You said you were leaving Provincetown tomorrow and had no plans for the rest of the summer," Paul continued, "and the weather's been great."

Terence smiled, remembering their conversation. Between the wine and Paul's friendliness and unassuming manner, Terence realized he had confided some very personal information.

"Well, it's a little sudden—" he paused again.

"If there's one thing I've learned," said Paul, becoming suddenly serious, "it's to be spontaneous. Life's too short."

Terence looked away, embarrassed, and found himself staring into his wineglass at the tilting, swirling red liquid drawing translucent veils along the bowl.

"All you need are some serious beach clothes," Paul persisted, sensing victory, "and we could pick those up in

Provincetown. Also you and Robert are about the same size, so if there's anything else you need —" he looked at Robert.

"We'd love to have you," said Robert.

✳

The water had receded out of sight. Shafts of sunlight fell through gaps in the clouds, lighting up the sand, which lay wet and glistening and speckled with stones. Children played where the water had been, unaware of impending doom. The waves, he knew, were gathering in the distance. They would come soon, very soon, and it would be as if the clouds had fallen upon the earth. There would be no way of escape...

✳

Brilliant morning light awakened Terence from his dream. He rose and went to the window, pushing back the curtains. For a moment he was blinded by the violence of the morning light. He stood with his eyes closed and his arms spread out holding the curtains apart, feeling the light sear his naked body. He opened his eyes and vision gradually returned. The dunes behind the cottage slowly appeared and filled with color. Blue seeped into the sky, and the pale wafer of sun at the edge of a cloud swelled, becoming incandescent. He pushed the window open and the ocean air blew in with a heavy sigh, cool and caressing. Turning, he rubbed his eyes and looked down at his body, which appeared as an afterimage, gradually darkening as it solidified.

"Good morning."

Startled, Terence moved instinctively to cover himself. Robert turned away, going into the kitchen.

"Coffee?" he called back, perfunctorily.

"Yes," said Terence, pulling on a pair of jeans, "please."

"It'll be a great day for swimming," came Robert's voice from the kitchen, "would you like to go?"

"Sure, I love to swim."

164

✳

Not a cloud marred the perfect emptiness of the steel blue sky. The sand burned with the sun's radiance, which reflected off the shifting, broken mirrors of the water's surface. Silver lips of whitecaps opened and closed in the offing, moving toward the shore obliquely, rocking, swelling, suddenly diaphanous, green waves breaking upon the cupped hands of the shore. The wind blew from unseen, exotic places. Gulls drifted and plunged, their thin voices barely audible above the booming ocean.

Paul sat on the beach watching Terence as he approached, dripping with seawater.

"You're really dark! I'm jealous," he observed, as Terence shook water from his head and arms, spraying Paul.

"The water's great! Maybe Robert and I can get one of those big, black tire tubes and take you out."

"I'm so pale all the time. I wish I could be in the sun more."

"This is a great setup," said Terence, admiring the lean-to which he and Robert had constructed with poles and sheets. He crawled under and sat beside Paul. "You look like Lawrence of Arabia under this thing."

Paul's gaze passed over him.

"Is Robert still out there?"

"Yeah. He really loves the ocean, doesn't he?"

"That's because he's a Pisces."

"And what are you?"

"A Scorpio."

"My birthday's September fourth."

"Virgo."

"So what does that mean?"

Paul smiled sardonically.

"You're a virgin."

"A virgin!" Terence exclaimed, laughing.

A gust of wind came up suddenly. The sheets flapped, straining against the poles. The light that reflected off them lit up Paul's face, and Terence noticed for the first time that his eyes were a deep blue-green. Paul lifted his hand to shield his eyes from the sun and gazed out over the ocean.

"Here comes Robert."

Terence turned to look, but part of the sheet had come loose, obscuring his view with pale and violent undulations as it strained to tear itself free.

✳

That night a heavy mist blew off the ocean. Robert loved walking the beach in the fog and asked Terence to join him. They walked along a path through the dunes behind the cottage. The sound of the ocean grew suddenly louder, and on the beach the sand sucked at their feet, slowing them. The dense fog had become a presence that swallowed the earth and water. With no points of reference Terence experienced a sensation of vertigo. He looked behind him and saw only the pale silhouette of the dunes, illuminated by streetlights in the distance. The ocean roared and echoed unseen along vast distances. All at once he was overwhelmed by its immensity, and a terrible anxiety seized him.

"Robert!" he called out, "I can't see you!"

"Over here!"

A ghostly figure emerged from the mist as he walked in the direction of the voice. He stood beside Robert, who was watching dark waves forming out of the fog where the ocean had been. Deliberately, hypnotically, they unfolded, laying themselves down, veil after veil, upon the steaming sand.

"Beautiful," said Terence, watching Robert watch the waves.

"I'm glad you stayed," said Robert, and after a pause, "Paul needs to have good people around."

They walked for a time in silence along the beach.

Terence stared out the windows at the bay. In the dark, light rippled across the water's surface, exposing the flow of the tide. His gaze followed the blinking lights of boats, and the slow, even movement of the lighthouse beacon. They had driven into Provincetown for dinner and were sitting over after-dinner coffee, lulled by wine and pleasant conversation.

"Let's go dancing," said Paul, abruptly.

Robert looked at him with surprise.

"You can't dance," said Robert.

"I used to be able to," Paul said, smiling at Terence. "Maybe I want to pick somebody up."

Robert laughed, and took Paul's hand under the table.

"I'm game if you are," said Terence.

Robert looked at Terence for a moment and then at Paul. He squeezed his hand.

"Okay. Let's go."

The bar was just beginning to fill. They took a table after getting drinks.

"That one's a cowboy, but only as a pastime — look at the perfect jeans and spotless boots."

"There's his lover. You can tell they're married, because he took a cigarette from him and then turned away as if he didn't know him."

"What about the bartender?"

"Very cute. He'll make a lot on tips."

"The one that just left the bar," said Paul, leaning toward Terence.

"Yeah?"

"He's into boys."

Terence looked at Paul, their faces almost touching.

"How can you tell?"

167

A sardonic smile formed on Paul's face. "I know the type."

The music became louder and more rhythmic as people crowded into the bar. Terence asked Robert to dance. Strobe lights flashed and bodies moved in pairs to the pulsing beat of the music. The dance floor became jammed with dancers.

Terence tried to speak above the music. He put his hand on Robert's arm, and when he leaned toward him to hear what he was saying, Terence's lips inadvertently touched his ear, sending a wave of desire through him. In that moment he felt the full impact of his desire for Robert. They moved away from and toward one another again and again as bodies surged all around them. Suddenly the music faltered, lulling into a slow and melancholy ballad. Almost everyone began leaving the dance floor. The few couples who remained lost themselves in the reverie of each other's arms, swaying in slow circles. Terence looked at Robert — he wanted to hold him.

"Shall we sit this one out?" said Robert.

"Why aren't you two dancing?" asked Paul, as they returned.

"We were," replied Robert.

Paul smiled at Terence. "I'd dance with you if I could."

"I'd like that. Do you think you could manage a slow dance?"

Without a word Paul stood up, almost losing his balance.

"See what too much liquor does," said Terence, taking Paul's hand and leading him onto the dance floor.

"The wine helps my shakes," he said, putting his arms around Terence. Terence felt a wave of pleasure, followed by repugnance. He could sense the presence of the disease, but Paul's sensuality was overwhelming. Terence was struck by how a man's embrace was more telling than a kiss as Paul pressed himself closer. He drew back and looked at Paul. The shifting lights glazed his features, and Terence had the impression that he was seeing Paul as he was before the monster had begun to possess him. He put his cheek against Paul's, and as he closed his eyes he saw the delicate, shining petals of a porcelain flower, unfolding in an endless night.

Robert watched them dance and remembered Paul and his first date when they had held each other and danced in just the same way. And he thought about the year that followed. Will he come back to me? He had been so naive that first time, standing in the doorway, and then sitting on the porch, convinced he was waiting for the sun to set, but in fact waiting for Paul. The sun, he remembered, had sunk at last, that first time, its light flattening on the horizon, a bloodline of light extinguishing between two dull and immovable masses: the dark silhouette of the hills and the deepening violet of the sky.

He was used to unfaithful lovers by then, but Paul was different — he cared. He was just too young ... too young ... too young. Like a bell tolling vespers. Too young, his friends had told him. Paul had actually suggested three-ways. That made Robert sad, but not angry. He knew Paul wasn't suggesting it to hurt him; he wanted Robert to be happy, to share everything with him. He's so naive when it comes to love, Robert had thought; and yet he couldn't help doubting himself. Maybe he was the naive one, the proud and stubborn one.

But he loved Paul, and as long as he kept coming back, Robert would keep forgiving him.

※

Early in the morning, just before he awoke, Terence had a vivid dream. He was alone, walking down a slope toward the ocean. There were bare trees partially obscuring his view. It was winter, but he felt no sensation of cold. As he descended toward the beach he noticed dark clouds forming over the water on the horizon. Suddenly he realized that the clouds were actually waves. All along the beach as far as he could see giant waves were rolling onto the shore, breaking violently. Directly ahead of him one enormous wave shattered with a roar into great masses of white spray. He was exhilarated, but also apprehensive. With each approach the waves seemed to reach closer, and break with greater fury. He didn't move, despite mounting fear. He was fascinated, and though he felt there was enough time to retreat to safety, he had the distinct feeling that time was running out.

✳

The following evening Terence made dinner. Robert had gone out alone for a walk on the beach.

"I like listening to classical music when I cook," said Terence, inserting a tape into the portable tape player on top of the refrigerator. "You don't mind, do you?"

"No," replied Paul, smiling. "I like a lot of things."

"Do you mind if I ask you a personal question?"

"Not at all," said Paul.

"I've been having the strangest feelings lately. I don't know — I've got this thing about intuition —" he paused. "Are you and Robert having problems?"

Paul was silent for a few moments. "It's really been hard for both of us, if that's what you mean," he said finally. "When I have a good day I like to pretend there's nothing wrong, and do things I can't usually do. It's like being in a fantasy world — the usual rules don't mean anything most of the time."

"I'm sorry," said Terence. "I've just been kind of confused lately, and I— " he paused, "—I had a friend—" He paused again and sighed, exhaling the memory. "I really like you two, and I just don't want to create any more problems than you already have."

"You're not creating any problems," said Paul. "It's great having you here. We don't have many friends — it's amazing, all the people who stopped seeing us when they found out I had AIDS; even some of our so-called close friends. We never had a weekend here by ourselves in the past. It's funny how people can change so fast."

"I just don't want to see anyone get hurt."

"It's all right—" Paul assured him. He embraced Terence, whispering enigmatically, "—and don't worry about Robert."

Terence pulled away and stared at him — he felt suddenly afraid.

"It's all right," Paul repeated.

✳

The next morning Terence rose early. He dressed quickly and left a note saying he would return later in the day. He needed to spend some time alone to sort things out. He sensed that he was getting involved with two people, but the one he wanted seemed out of reach. Paul's illness added a horrible twist to an already complicated situation. Terence was confused by his talk with Paul the previous evening; he had begun to feel guilty. He felt no fear, however, being physically close to Paul. His only fear was his desire for Robert and the chasm which it had opened in his emotions; a rift in his psyche that grew wider each day, threatening to swallow him.

Later in the day, when he returned to the cottage, he saw that Robert's car was gone. Once inside he experienced an inexplicable feeling of oppression. He changed his clothes and went out again.

The beach was almost deserted. The edges of receding waves wept with foam, sweeping in long arcs across the sand. The sky was clear except for clouds that shrouded the horizon. The obscurity filled Terence with uneasiness. He walked on and on, attempting to escape from his troubling thoughts.

A couple of hours later he returned to the still-deserted cottage. There was a note on top of the one he had left that morning. He realized that it must have been there when he returned earlier, but he hadn't noticed it.

The note was written by Robert. Paul was very sick and had to be taken to the hospital in Hyannis, about a half-hour drive south. He didn't know if or when he would be back that day. The note's brevity as much as its content disturbed Terence. He began pacing the living room trying to decide what he should do. Suddenly he realized that he had been so preoccupied with his thoughts during the day that he hadn't eaten since breakfast, and hunger was causing him to fade out. He made a sandwich and drank several glasses of wine while re-reading the letter. He had the strange feeling that there was a hidden message evading him.

"It must be my imagination," he sighed, "I'm so tired."

Without undressing he lay down upon the unmade sofa bed.

✳

Slowly, silently, a wall, whose gray-speckled skin expanded with each moment into something gigantic, rose up before him. Long, white streaks like spittle formed on its surface. Gradually it became lighter; blue, turquoise, pale green. His gaze followed its movement up, higher and higher. At the top bubbles, every color of the rainbow, oozed out of foam. It was a wave. At the very moment that he recognized it he awoke. His heart was pounding; he was suffocating. He jumped from the sofa bed and went to the window, pushing it open. His panic slowly subsided. The night was cool. He could hear the slow and even pulse of the ocean in the distance.

"Are you okay?"

"Jesus!"

He whirled around. Robert was sitting in a chair in a corner of the room.

"Sorry, I thought you'd see the light when you woke up."

Terence sighed, leaning against the window frame. His head was aching. After a few moments he went back to the sofa bed and sat on the edge.

Robert got up from the chair and went over to Terence. He sat down next to him and began relating what had happened that day. He spoke almost in a whisper. Terence couldn't focus on what Robert was saying. Strangely, he felt himself descending into the dream again. He heard only phrases out of context, words, names.

"Cape Cod Hospital," Terence repeated, groping his way back, "where—"

Robert's voice faltered. He was crying.

Terence felt himself sinking. He put his arm around Robert to comfort him, but also to keep himself from going under. The contact sobered him.

"Robert," he whispered, "Robert, I'm so sorry—"

He felt the weight of Robert's body pressing suddenly against him. They were both sinking now.

✳

It seemed that every few moments he was opening his eyes. In one of those moments it was dark, in another it was morning. He couldn't remember clearly what had actually happened or what he had dreamt. Images and words had appeared as objects on bits of broken mirror, moving across his line of vision, vividly, and in rapid succession, too rapid for him to be able to determine whether any of them were actual events. He lay perfectly still watching the shadows evaporate into the pale morning twilight. Robert lay sleeping beside him.

＊

Paul returned on the weekend. He was thinner and very pale. The disease was drawing him steadily inward. He gave Terence a wistful smile when he entered the cottage. They embraced, and in that moment Terence realized how much he cared for Paul. He also realized that his memories were becoming a disease, and he was overcome with a feeling of hopelessness. He held Paul tightly, he wanted to comfort him, to protect him. When they parted, Paul's sardonic smile had returned; defiance had found its way back, but Terence found the abruptness of the transformation somehow disconcerting.

During lunch Terence kept looking at Robert for a sign, but he had become withdrawn. When Terence asked Paul about the hospital, his responses were so terse that he dropped the subject after a few minutes. An uncomfortable silence ensued.

"How's the swimming been?" asked Paul.

"There've been warnings issued against swimming for the last week because of a serious undertow," replied Terence.

"I thought there was always an undertow?"

"I guess so, but two people have drowned. Some meteorologist or other was explaining how it has to do with the wind and wave patterns. I don't exactly understand it."

He glanced at Robert again. He was far off, lost in his thoughts.

＊

Terence picked up another flat stone and flung it at the waves. Desire caressed him like the claw of a beast in a ⁻ silken glove. When he watched the waves gathering in the offing he imagined himself floating, a thousand hands holding him aloft, an undulating cushion carrying him on an unknown course, until, reaching the inevitable shore, the hands once again became waves, transforming into crescents; translucent, delicate pieces of blue silk, the glove flung off in a swift and shattering metamorphosis. In this way the waves reminded Terence of the men he had known. He felt dangerous. Could he love Robert? He always drew men to him with the intensity of his desire, but feared the catastrophe of their embraces. He was swept up in desire, riding the waves with exhilaration; but panic had suddenly seized him, and he found himself floundering in self-denial. The inevitable question rose up, a wall in his path: did he love Robert? The rose-amber glow of his fantasies was fading rapidly as the question began to stalk him.

He walked on for some time. The sun lingered interminably over the horizon, burnishing the dunes. Marsh grass, bent low by the wind, scintillated in golden light. Burnt wisps of clouds hung in the air over the sun, as if adding weight to its descent. The fading of the light and changing of the waves, the peculiar emptiness of the beach, all conspired to fill him with melancholy. He longed to hold Robert again, and in that moment, as if the fading of the light had given him a new vision, he knew he had to be in love.

✳

Robert was sitting on the sofa when Terence returned to the cottage. "Paul's sleeping."

Terence paused before going to sit beside him.

"I don't know if I can go through with it," Robert said, absently.

Terence felt a strange sensation as Robert spoke, as if Robert were talking in his sleep. So he thought Paul would have to go back to the hospital.

"If he has to go back, what else can you do? Maybe you should take him to Boston. He would probably get better care there. I could go with you."

Robert looked at him with an anguished expression, and then began to cry. Terence put his arms around him.

"I'm sorry," Robert sobbed, "I can't help it. It's out of my hands now, and I wish—"

After a few moments Robert drew back and looked at Terence, whose eyes were glazed with tears. All of Terence's hopes and fears were confirmed in Robert's look. He rushed up and over Terence, giving himself and pulling back, again and again. Terence lay beneath him, now covered, now exposed, while in the distance the sand groaned, holding the water, holding the air; and the waves came in, without hesitation, fulfilling the unknown and unknowable purpose of the forces impelling them, row after row, now gently, now violently, breaking and receding in an eternal caress upon the earth.

✳

Some time later Robert arose from Terence's embrace.

"What's the matter?" Terence whispered, trying not to break the spell.

"I thought I heard Paul."

He left the sofa bed and went into the bedroom. Terence sat up, listening. A small square of moonlight lay upon the floor. He could hear nothing but the steady breathing of the ocean in the distance. Closing his eyes he saw the dunes in shadow behind the cottage, the dark expanse of beach beyond, and, farther still, the waves gleaming softly in broken patches beneath the moon.

"Terence—"

He opened his eyes, expecting to see Robert standing before him. He was alone.

"Terence—"

Rising, naked, he went to the bedroom door, pausing for a moment before going in. The room was streaked with moonlight. The twisted sheets on the bed glowed softly. Robert held Paul, who lay on his back gazing inscrutably

176

toward the ceiling. Robert was smiling across a great distance. Without hesitation Terence stepped forward through veils of shadow and light. His feet made no sound. When he lifted the sheet Paul looked up at him. Terence felt as if he was descending into the great, unknown expanse of the boy's eyes. He lay down next to him. He put his arm across the boy's chest and his right leg over the boy's right leg and pressed his face against the boy's face, feeling a smile against his lips, and formed exactly the other half of Paul's desire. The three lay motionless, forming a single entity like some Hindu statue, while all around them the night dissolved slowly, almost imperceptibly, into paleness.

✳

The next morning Robert was a different person. Distracted, he paced the kitchen nervously. He appeared, to Terence, like a caged animal.

"We *have* to take him to the hospital," Terence repeated.

He couldn't understand why Robert was hesitating. Paul had awakened them, shaking with a fever. They gave him aspirin and applied compresses to his forehead and wrists. When Robert went into the kitchen to change the water in the basin, Terence followed him.

"I know how awful it is for him there, but you've got to—"

"No hospital!"

Terence was shocked by the unexpected outburst. "You're going to let him die then," he said flatly. He was becoming angry. Robert stared at him with a pained expression.

"I can't stay here and do nothing," Terence said, decisively. He went into the living room to call the hospital. Robert followed him. As Terence began to dial, Robert went to the wall and pulled out the telephone cord. Terence looked at him in disbelief.

"What are you doing! Have you lost your mind!"

"I'm sorry. I can't let you interfere."

"Interfere! What are you talking about?"

"I—" Robert's expression changed suddenly. "I'm sorry — I'm sorry — I never should have—" His eyes were strained with an effort to speak, but his mouth became rigid.

Terence's anger turned to fear. "Never should have what?"

"Never should have involved you."

"Never should have gotten involved with me. Is that what you mean?"

Robert stared at him helplessly.

"Please tell me," Terence implored.

"I think you'd better go now," replied Robert, without emotion.

He seemed to have turned to stone but for his eyes, which were filled with anguish. Terence turned away without a word and left the cottage.

＊

Robert remained motionless after Terence was gone, and didn't move until the sound of his car had died away. He felt sad, but another sensation had begun to take possession of him. His heart beat faster, and there was a tingling in his spine that slowly spread throughout his body. A weight was lifting. Nothing was holding him now: no fear, no obligation, no law, no desire, he was free. He went into the bedroom. Paul was lying curled up on the bed. His eyes met Robert's when he entered the room. Robert went to the desk and opened a drawer from which he removed a container of pills. A wave of sadness rose up and threatened to overwhelm him. He hesitated. His eyes were fixed upon the container, which blurred through the coming of tears. The sadness stabbed at his heart, as his thoughts, his hopes, his dreams, crashed, sending ripples of despair throughout the room. The curtains stirred for a moment and then hung limp. He sat at the writing table and wrote what he had been unable to say. He went to the bed. Paul could not speak, but there was a question in his look. Robert took him into his arms.

Light reflected off the pale walls. The room glowed softly. The curtains pulsed against a breeze synchronized perfectly to the sound of waves rushing up onto the sand in the distance. The sky was a pale blue dome, exactly the color of Robert's eyes. He looked down into Paul's face, whom he held in his arms like a pietà. Paul's eyes were glazed; he seemed to have ceased to look outward, yet his spirit, a wisp of smoke, still fluttered within his wasted body. Time passed. Minutes? Hours? A cloud moved across the sky of Robert's eyes. The curtains stood motionless. The air was still. The ocean sighed between pulses. Teardrops fell upon Paul's face, pale and glassy, and rolled softly down his cheek and onto his shoulder. How strange that a dead boy should appear to be weeping. Robert drew the body into an embrace and cried, rocking back and forth as if putting a child to sleep. The curtains stirred. A breeze blew in through the open window from the ocean, which sounded more urgent now, pushing the letter to the edge of the writing table, where it tipped back and forth for a moment before fluttering noiselessly to the floor.

✳

Terence drove too fast through the narrow back streets and almost went off the road at a sharp turn. His head throbbed with anger and confusion.

"Where am I going!" he cried, hitting the steering wheel. "I don't even know where I'm going!"

He pulled off the road and tried to collect his thoughts. He didn't know where the police station was; he knew where the hospital was, but it seemed too far. He decided to call an ambulance. He drove into the nearest driveway. No one answered when he rang the doorbell. He rang again. He looked at the next house over — no car in the driveway. Suddenly he was aware of how silent it was. There was no traffic, and he couldn't hear the ocean to which he had grown so accustomed. The ocean. It came to him out of the silence: the ocean. He saw Robert standing before him again. There was something very wrong in his look, his voice, his whole manner.

"I shouldn't have left," he said aloud.

As he spoke he felt as if he was waking from a dream. All the tormenting thoughts fled at once except for one: he had to go back.

*

The curtains of the bedroom billowed restlessly. A pale light filled the room. The letter on the floor inched forward each time the curtains stirred. The ocean sighed incessantly in the distance. And just over the dunes at the back of the cottage a man was walking slowly across the beach toward the water. Sea gulls drifted overhead in the clear air of the radiant day, their cries floating down to the earth, agonized and melancholy.

Terence rushed into the bedroom and stopped abruptly. Paul lay motionless on the bed. The curtains stirred; the letter touched Terence's foot. He felt the whole weight of his life press down upon him as he stooped to pick it up.

I know you will probably never be able to understand why I did what I did. The hospital was a terrible place for Paul — he hated it. We knew they couldn't help him. And he was afraid for me. He knew I couldn't make it without him. He wanted me to have someone to get me through the bad times that we knew were coming. I agreed to his plan for me to get together with you. I really didn't want someone else to be involved in this, please believe me. I'm sorry. I felt myself becoming too involved, but I couldn't for Paul's sake. He really loved you. Can you believe that? He loved us both—

180

The words blurred through Terence's tears. He crumpled the paper into his fist. Suddenly a gust of wind blew into the room. He glanced at the flapping curtains straining to free themselves. He could hear the waves. He ran from the room and out of the house. Within moments he was on the dunes looking over the beach. In the distance, just past the point where the earth met the water, where the light burned silver upon the waves, he saw a figure. A shock jolted him forward. The sand sucked at his feet slowing him, as in a dream.

"You bastard, Robert! No!"

He fell, cursing the sand that seemed part of the conspiracy. He was panting as he lifted himself up and continued to run. The first wave struck him. He felt no sensation of cold as he entered the water. The waves pushed him back. He strained against each swell, but Robert was out of sight now. The gulf between them, Terence realized, could not be breached.

The ocean had lifted Robert up from the earth. There is no more struggling, he thought, no more crashing of waves (far off he could hear them, whispering among themselves). He never imagined it would be like this, so silent, so gentle, like being rocked to sleep under a pale blue sky.

The waves surrendered to the earth while clouds rose up and mottled the sky gray. Marsh grass shuddered along the lips of dunes facing the surf, where fluttering stones, smoothed perfect, tumbled in broken waves, etching the sand with hieroglyphics that no one can decipher, erasing them and writing again and again. All the while the sun moved in perfect increments, burning a path of brilliance across the sky, where, each day, it draws a line parallel to the one before it. Gasping, the wind blew, driving the water before it. Wave after wave rose up and tumbled down, one after another, as if to say: I am here now I am gone.

Luke Dedrick — Burnt things

When school started in Winfield County that year, a rumor was going around that the man who lived at rural route four near Klamath Pond, where the kids liked to fish and swim, was a homosexual.

"You mean he's a faggot?" Harlan Frakes, a boy in Calvin Eddy's homeroom, said, his mouth twisted with disgust. "Me and my brother have been fishin' over there!"

Once the rumor began circulating, cruel things happened to Hunter Klamath. Someone with a rifle shot through the window at a figure — a sewing-room dummy with the flannel for a shirt pinned to it. Hunter swung a rake at two boys who stoned his milk cow. One night someone polluted his pond with boxes of laundry soap; for more than a week Hunter scooped out the poisoned, bloated catfish. Finally the worst thing of all happened: someone burned down his house.

In that part of Kansas there are at least a dozen farms about a mile apart. The Eddys hardly knew this man who lived closest to them, but because he seemed friendless, they invited Hunter to stay in their house. The night of the fire Hunter Klamath and his dog moved in. He brought a gunnysack of the burnt things with him.

For almost three weeks Hunter slept in Calvin's bedroom, and Calvin slept on the couch. Calvin would often wake up to the muffled sounds coming from behind his bedroom door. He was fifteen and couldn't remember the last time he had cried; he thought it strange that a man in his forties would still cry. He thought of school and how he would force laughter at the stories about the stranger staying in his house. He felt embarrassed when another boy asked him: "Do you know how two men do it?"

Hunter's dog avoided the Eddy's dog, and it was especially afraid of their billy goat. In the evening and throughout the night Hunter's dog whined and barked on the back porch. It never seemed to sleep. Calvin didn't complain to his parents about the noises. At night or sometimes early in the mornings, he'd squint in the dark as Hunter tiptoed past the couch and opened the back door. He'd listen to his low voice soothe the dog to a brief silence, and somehow Calvin felt soothed too.

The first day of fall brought a brief Indian summer. Hunter asked to use the garden hose in the backyard. "I made you promise to make yourself at home," Mrs. Eddy gently scolded. "You know you don't have to ask." And Calvin watched through the screen door, as Hunter held his dog close. "Good boy, good boy," he repeated as he tried again to wash away the smell of the smoke.

Mrs. Eddy tried repeatedly to wash the smoke from Hunter's clothes. She told him she'd had to use bleach on all of his laundry, even the colors. His blue jeans turned cloudy white, and his red nightshirt faded to pink. Hunter said he didn't mind; there was very little conversation between the Eddys and their houseguest.

Sometimes he'd take the dog and walk over to his own farm. "I need to start assessing the damage," he explained to Mrs. Eddy. The fire marshal from Wichita had told him that the house would have to be completely rebuilt. On those mornings when he was gone, Mrs. Eddy opened Calvin's bedroom windows, but the smell of smoke remained in their house.

Quite suddenly, toward the end of fall, Hunter and his dog left the Eddys' farm. He thanked the family, and though his house had been condemned, he said he was moving back to begin rebuilding.

Soon after, a baby-faced sheriff's deputy visited the Eddys and questioned them about Hunter. "Ma'am, there's a rumor going around. At least I hope it's just a rumor."

"What exactly is the rumor?" Mrs. Eddy asked.

"I know you folks put up Hunter Klamath for a while after the fire." He looked down at his shoes with vacant eyes. "I guess you've talked to your boy about him." The deputy waited ready to scribble on a pad in front of him. "He didn't bother your boy, did he?"

At first the rumor enraged Mr. and Mrs. Eddy, then numbed them into a kind of embarrassment. Mrs. Eddy scoured the house from top to bottom to rid it once and for all of the smell of smoke. The subject of homosexuality was never broached, even between themselves.

"I can still smell something in my room," Calvin announced one morning at breakfast. Mrs. Eddy informed her husband that she'd read an article in *Woman's Day* about teenage sons. "They commonly have what are called 'olfactory hallucinations,'" she said. She assured her husband and Calvin that the smell of smoke was gone.

Calvin couldn't describe the smell. During the nights in the early winter he was awakened and then aroused again and again. It was in his blankets and pillow: a trace of smoke, his own fervor, and the smell of a man he hardly knew. When he masturbated, during those seconds between his last hard strokes and an orgasm, he allowed his fantasy to take on the face and body of that man.

184

Once, in the darkness in his first hour of sleep, Calvin heard the quiet ghost of Hunter's soft cry. There was an instant when he thought he knew he was dreaming. Calvin talked in his sleep; "I smell the fire," he mumbled. He woke himself with his own voice and wondered if these were the half-beginnings of a nightmare. His right arm underneath him was numb, and he let it drop to the floor. As blood rushed through his arm he felt something coarse. Calvin knew that there were burnt things under his bed.

He was wide awake now. He sat up and pulled out Hunter's forgotten gunnysack from under his bed; it reminded him of the bulky bags of baseball equipment from his P.E. class. He turned the bag upside down and poured its contents out on the bed. There was a ball and a catcher's mitt. There were shoes, and at least one in every pair had been ruined by the fire. A camera made out of Bakelite was as big as a shoe box. A leather-bound photo album was half-full of pictures. He opened a blackened cigar box, and inside was a man's gold wedding ring, a wristwatch without a band or a crystal, a folded, brittle bird's wing, probably that of an owl, and a brown photograph that had blistered and curled. On the back of the picture was written, "Affectionately, Ben." There was also a dark blob of plastic the size of a clenched fist, once separate things that had melted together.

Calvin looked carefully through the photo album. There were snapshots of Hunter when he was smaller and younger. He was swimming in the pond in one picture and waving from the seat of a tractor in another. Calvin removed and kept a photograph of Hunter and another man standing with their shirts off squinting at the sun. They had their arms around each other. He recognized "Ben" from the picture in the cigar box.

Calvin felt a sudden clarity to his recent worries and desires. He choked back a sob, but held on to the guilt growing quietly like a tumor in his chest. He hadn't been part of the scheme to poison the pond, and he didn't shoot through Hunter's window. But after Harlan Frakes and his brother poured gasoline on the floor of the house, Calvin lit the match. He thought of that rumor they had spread about Hunter Klamath. He knew that, had it been about himself, it would have been the truth, not a rumor at all.

The next morning brought sunlight and swirling snow at the same time. Calvin felt an uncertain hope and was suddenly in a hurry for this winter to be part of the past. He skipped breakfast, and after shoveling the front path he walked the mile to Hunter's farm, dragging the gunnysack behind him. Hunter's house stood between the pond and a field of frozen stunted wheat. For a while he remained motionless on the road away from the face of the house. Occasionally he'd look up and count the blackbirds swooping across the white sky.

On the front porch the familiar charred smell was stronger. Calvin waited for a long time, and then he knocked on the door. He waited a bit, knocked hard again, and some snow slid off the roof behind him. He let the bag fall on its side and reached for the doorknob. Calvin was not surprised that it was unlocked.

In the hallway he couldn't see much until his eyes grew accustomed to the dark. Then, he stepped farther into the house. He would always remember what he saw. There were no signs of the rebuilding of Hunter's house; to Calvin it looked like a tiny frozen black forest. The walls were burned away, so he could see all the way to the back. Most of the beams were exposed, as were the springs in a sofa, a chair, and a large bed. Water dripped from the tips of long icicles that hung from holes in the ceiling. Through a larger hole snow was falling. In the corners small drifts of white formed where the fire had burned away all color. When he stepped sideways, his left foot broke through the floor. Grasping for support, he set a charred rocker in motion that rocked back and forth and then collapsed. In the cold air

Calvin's senses were numb; he no longer noticed the bitter smell left by the fire. He felt his empty stomach tighten as he took in the destruction he had created.

He finally pulled himself up on a beam in the floor. He estimated its path under his feet and followed it to the kitchen. He could hear a dog barking outside. From the kitchen window he could see Hunter and his dog standing at the edge of the pond. In what seemed to Calvin to be a spur-of-the-moment decision, Hunter stepped gently out on to the ice; then, as if on a dare, he shuffled halfway across the frozen pond to a bump on the surface. The dog leapt into the air and barked, afraid to follow. Calvin watched closely, then smiled when he heard a click. It wasn't a crack forming, but Hunter plucking a quill from a porcupine suspended in ice.

When Calvin left for home he took the bag of burnt things with him. He thought of it as an excuse to return to the farm. As he walked in the snow, he searched for some kind of a penance. He envisioned there would be a day when he and Hunter would have a long conversation; at his age, in his mind, Calvin believed a lot would happen on that day. Maybe he could stay on the farm and help rebuild it. They would both stand up to the abuse and vandalism. He believed that he too would be brave enough to walk out on that frozen pond. He dreamed of the coming summer and Hunter teaching him how to swim. With the sun on their chests and their arms around each other's shoulders, they'd have their picture taken together.

After that he went to Hunter's farm almost every Saturday. He would watch for him and his dog from inside the crumbling house. Sometimes Hunter would sit for an hour in his dark red Buick warming the engine. Once when Hunter had driven away, Calvin went into the barn and found the small room in a corner where a space heater kept them warm at night. At first he left some of the things from the bag on the porch of the house, but they were left untouched. Throughout the winter and early spring the floors in the house slowly rotted and even the front porch stairs caved in. One day he brought some food and the photo album and put them on the pallet where Hunter slept in the barn. Next to a vase of porcupine quills he placed the owl's wing.

The spring was slow in coming. Showers finally dispelled Winfield County's long cold wave and the last crusts of muddy ice. The pond was clear again, but the boys from the school didn't come back to fish. Calvin had marked the first Saturday in May as a day for a proper confrontation; when the day came the sky was slate gray.

As he approached Hunter's farm, it began to pour. He ran and pressed his back against the barn. He wondered if Hunter would hear his knock. All of a sudden the wide, wooden door rumbled sideways along its runner, and Hunter stood staring at the soaked figure in the rain.

Calvin detected some fear in Hunter's eyes, but it quickly faded. "You've been here before," Hunter said slowly. "You've been bringing my things back, haven't you, Cal?"

And he liked the soothing voice calling him Cal. He hesitated, then tried blurting out the carefully chosen words he'd been saving, but they wouldn't come. He could barely utter even the simplest words.

"I started the fire. I'm the one who burned your house down," he muttered into the rain. To his own ears he sounded weak and hoarse. In his drenched clothes Calvin stood still for a moment. He wanted to explain his guilt and his self-loathing, but he could only stutter. He felt certain that Hunter was the only one like him, the only one who could forgive him. "I didn't do it to hurt you," Calvin cried. He wiped the rain from his face. "I did it because I didn't want to be like you! But, I know I am like you. Do you understand me?" Hunter nodded, pretending to understand, but Calvin knew he hadn't reached him. In his mind all of the conversations he'd had with his imaginary lover had been so clear and simple. He stepped backward, away from the barn. His heart felt empty. As he turned to run away he saw Hunter drag the gunnysack out of a puddle and into the barn. He thought he heard the dog barking, but he wasn't sure. He guessed it was just the rain slapping hard against the earth.

*

On the Fourth of July, when a young boy disappeared from his front yard in nearby Hutchinson, the baby-faced sheriff's deputy visited Hunter's farm. "Just checking any and all possibilities," he said. He circled the house and looked in a broken window at the charred interior. "You ever gonna do anything with this place?"

Not long after that Hunter and his dog left that part of Kansas. Now, when Calvin thought of Hunter, he imagined him to be as far away as the skyscrapers, or the oceans, or the stars. Calvin hadn't been to the farm since that day it had rained. On the day he went back it hit ninety or higher. The farm seemed to be a different place; nearly a year of wind had blown through the structure, and it was reduced to mostly a shell leaning to one side. He noticed some color had finally returned to the farmhouse — yellow weeds popping up through the holes in the porch and emerald green clumps of moss growing on the black timber.

Larry Duplechan

Presently in the past

I dreamed about Martin last night. Odd. He hadn't popped up in a dream — not that I remembered, anyway — in a year or more. No doubt, it had to do with seeing that boy in the bookstore the other day, leaning against the magazine stand, flipping through the current *Advocate MEN*, looking so much like a 22- or 23-year-old Martin Waterson would have to look that I got a little head rush of adrenaline and nearly hurried over to him. Except by now, Martin, wherever he may sleep tonight, is *thirty*-three, not twenty-three. An "older guy," as that kid said: the cute young muffin who tried to get friendly with me at Mickey's last Saturday night, giving me the look and the smile and telling me how he *likes* older guys. Older guys. Seems just a week ago Thursday I was chicken.

A disturbing little habit I've noticed recently — forgetting my own age. Meeting people I assume are about my age, only to find they're five to ten years shy of about my age. Since thirty, memory has become quite the mischievous little gremlin. More and more, I find I'll forget the name of a good friend's latest significant other (John? Steve? Michael?), a man I'd met mere hours before; but suddenly, out of nowhere, my mind will serve up something twenty years old, clear as cable television, clean as a paper cut. Like that dream. There we were: Martin and me, sitting in the bleachers behind the far softball diamond at John C. Calhoun, as we often did, as we did the day he told me he was going away.

So naturally, I woke up with Martin on my mind, and I couldn't shake him all morning. The memories shoved their way to the front of my thoughts like rowdy teenagers in a theater queue, and I was in no mood to fight. I was minding my own business, waiting for the coffee to drip and the toaster to toast, when Martin says, "Who'm I doing?" and it's 1964. A year notable primarily for the beginning of my friendship with Martin, for the Beatles on the Sullivan show, and for the little song I heard Mark Baines — the tough kid from across the street, who swore, and who often called me a little shit-ass sissy to my face — singing, which I repeated within my mother's hearing, and which earned me a slap across the mouth the sting of which I remember to this day:

> In nineteen sixty-four
> My father was in the war;
> He pulled the trigger
> And shot a nigger
> In nineteen sixty-four.

"Don't you ever — *ever* — use that word again!" my mother commanded through clenched teeth. I seldom ever have.

"Who'm I doing?" Martin says. He's eight years old. He's pushing the tip of his freckle-spattered nose down into his upper lip. I'm already giggling behind my hand at Martin's often-repeated, sure-fire impression of Lady Bird

Johnson, even before Martin says, in his Los Angeles eight-year-old's version of a Texas drawl, "Lyndon ... Leeyundun..." It still makes me smile.

Later in the morning, I sat amid the unmanageable clutter that is my desk, less than two hours after breakfast and already lusting for lunch as I attempted the near-impossible — balancing my checkbook — searching in vain for $13.72 that seemed to have fallen through a tiny tear in the space-time continuum. Anything to postpone having to face the manuscript of my new novel, and my editor's infinitely irritating blue-penciled lines and loops. And then Martin bumps against my shoulder as we amble the last couple of blocks toward Sportsman's Park, which is situated equidistant between Martin's house and my own, and where we go to swim most weekdays during the summer.

"Why do people do things like that?" Martin asks. Asks me, himself, God maybe. We walk through a neighborhood of smallish one-story houses, where every other front lawn seems to have sprouted a For Sale sign like some huge mutant dandelion. Up until the past weekend, I had been too young, too naive to see that the signs announced the rapid, soon-as-we-can retreat of white residents, and the equally rapid encroachment of blacks. But over the weekend, ten minutes from the street where Martin and I walk, much of Watts was burned to embers. It had been all over the evening news, and even I — who hate to watch the news now, let alone at ten years old — watched: flaming buildings glowing bright orange against the dark of night. Angry dark faces, flashing white, white teeth. Negroes, the reporters kept saying. Negroes this, Negroes that. Negroes rioting. Negroes looting. Negroes chanting, "Burn, baby, burn."

Believe it or not, I had never thought of myself or my family as Negroes before. I don't recall my mother, my father, ever sitting me down and explaining that we were Negroes, and what that fact might mean to my life, and it had honestly never occurred to me. As far as I know, I was just me, we were just us. I had of course noticed that some people — myself included — were brown and some people were more of a pale-pink-and-orange, and so what? But now, now those brown people out in the streets, so close to our own house, in the same neighborhood as Mr. Lewis, my clarinet teacher; those brown people throwing bricks and stealing television sets and starting fires — they were Negroes Negroes Negroes, and so was I. During one of the newscasts, I had gone to the bathroom, looked at myself in the mirror, and whispered the word softly to myself: Negro.

And so the Monday morning after the weekend of burning, of smoke and sirens in the distance, I am beginning to realize why so many people — so many *white* people, it occurs to me — are selling their houses and moving away. And maybe why, even though Martin and I have been best friends for almost two whole years, I have been invited to his house only once. Martin's mother looked like Leave it to Beaver's mother, and she served us Chef-Boy-Ar-Dee pizza for lunch. When I asked Martin over to my house, there was always some reason why he couldn't that day. And after a few times, I stopped asking, and now Martin and I are best friends at school.

"Jesse," Martin says, "why do people do things like that?"

I turn to look at Martin. His fine, straight, copper-colored hair falling in bangs over his eyebrows — his father cuts his hair with scissors and a cereal bowl; the bony arm exposed by his short-sleeved t-shirt, its skin that impossible pale peculiar to the redhead. He has never seemed so different from me, so foreign to me before. I nearly say something like, "How should *I* know? I'm just a Negro." But Martin wouldn't know what I mean by that. I don't know what I mean by that. So I just shrug, and say, "Search *me*." I am barely ten years old, and I am only beginning to know why people do things like that.

By noon, I had given up all hope of finding the lost $13.72 and decided to concede defeat, take the Bank of America's word for it, and get on with my life. Frustrated and munchy and no more inclined to tackle my editor's marks than before, folding the checking statement around the thickish stack of last month's checks — I write checks for everything but parking meters — the image of the vegetarian burrito I had planned for lunch briefly gave way to a mental snapshot of Martin and me in Cub Scout uniforms, standing in line with the rest of Miss Muskat's fourth-grade class for school pictures. Me behind Martin, tugging gently at the corner of the yellow neckerchief pointing down between his shoulder blades, making silly little-boy physical contact with my friend, and feeling all right. During the three minutes it took to microwave my burrito, I watched Martin and me walking across the black asphalt yard at Calhoun Junior High, shoulder to shoulder, feeling safer together than we might have felt alone. We both limp just a little, each of us carrying his lunch money in his right shoe, never knowing when some big, unkempt boy with a curl in his lip and a small knife in his hip pocket might decide to shove one or both of us against the nearest classroom wall and pat us down.

Late in the afternoon, having procrastinated most of the daylight away with some half-assed stabs at housecleaning — hitting the bathroom "a lick and a promise," as my mother would say — I made myself a mug of tea and carried it and a couple of oatmeal cookies to the living room. I eased myself into the big blue armchair which is my favorite place to read or worry or just close my eyes and listen to Joni Mitchell CDs, and gave myself up to the memories, just sat back and invited them in. Ready to take my seat in those bleachers next to Martin one more time.

"We're moving," Martin says, not looking at me. His long, lanky body is bent in half, his elbows pointing into his knees, his voice an uncertain baritone, having already changed where mine had not, would not for nearly three more years. His small green eyes squint in the June sunshine, as he looks out across the schoolyard, where kids — most of them black — sit eating sack lunches, or stand talking, hands and arms and heads and hips in motion, or stroll in twos or groups. In a far corner, two tall boys are shoving at one another's chest, a few seconds and a couple of loud, challenging words away from a real fight.

"What?" My voice squeals like tires on a wet road. My face whips toward Martin, who still has not faced me. "You kidding?" I say. But I know he isn't. We have never discussed it, but I've known this was coming for a long time; certainly since the riots. At the same time, I have also imagined Martin and me just going on and on, indefinitely — at least through high school. Enduring the eighth grade without him seems unthinkable.

"My folks sold the house," Martin says. "I'm not even going to finish the semester."

My stomach has tightened; I'm afraid I may cry. I attempt twice to speak, but nothing comes. "Shoot," I say finally. As of the seventh grade, "shoot" is among the strongest expletives I ever utter. Martin finally faces me: his eyes and nose are red. He looks like I feel. "My folks," he says, "they don't like the neighborhood anymore." He looks away again.

"Why not?" I ask, although I know. "Too many niggers?"

Martin's head whips around. His reddened eyes are wild, his teeth bared in something like a snarl. "I never use that word!" He's almost shouting. "You know I never use that word!" By the look of his face, the desperate scratch in his voice, I am sure his parents have used that word. I had meant to hurt, but I'm still a little surprised that I have. Martin turns back toward the asphalt before asking, "You hate me?"

I sniff back some snot, do a big shrug, and quip, "'Course not. It's just your parents I can't stand." Leave it to me to pick the worst possible moment to do shtick.

Martin doesn't answer. I watch his profile as his chin begins to shake; as his face collapses into itself. Martin covers his face with his long hands, and he's crying. Through his palms I can hear wet breaths and a low hum from his throat.

"Martin!" I say through an aching throat. "I'm sorry!" My eyes sting with tears, and without thinking I lean toward Martin and encircle him with my arms — one up and over his shaking shoulders, the other under and around him. I hug him awkwardly, stroking the side of his head with my fingers, repeating, "I didn't mean it," and crying.

I got up from the chair and went to the bathroom to blow my nose. Like many, maybe most, artists, actors, writers, and schizophrenics, I carry all past hurts and heartaches just below the skin, where the smallest emotional pinprick can unleash them. Oh, I wasn't crying, exactly: just close enough to feel that little throb in the back of my throat, just close enough to make my sinuses fill. I leaned my behind against the bathroom sink and blew into two folded-over Kleenexes, making my wonted trumpeting-bull-elephant noise. Funny, I thought, the things you remember. And the things you don't. A line from *All about Eve*, but nonetheless true. Because the fact is I can't remember for the life of me how long Martin and I sat together crying. Or what was said after we were finished. Or how we got through the days until Martin left. My mind blanks. The film has broken, and the screen is left naked, blinding white.

I do remember that at some point after the time Martin and I cried, some boys accused me of having kissed Martin and teased me off and on for a few hours or a few days, until they eventually lost interest. Hardly a rare occurrence — small and bookish and more than slightly effeminate as I was, those who wanted to could usually find plenty to tease me about. I recall someone saying, "I saw you kissin' 'im. I saw you," and somebody else saying, "Where's your kissin' partner?" I remember that I ignored them, didn't answer, didn't deny it. And I remember wishing I had thought to kiss Martin.

Years later, it occurred to me that I had probably loved Martin, that he had likely been my first real love. That may well be: after all, I do still dream of him now and then, twenty years later. But then again, hindsight is notoriously revisionist. And as I've said, memory has become quite the mischievous little gremlin.

Virginia Witt — The angel of death on the Provincetown ferry

Elaine, the inquisitive one, noticed him first: a thin, elflike man squatting by the pier, reading a book. Unlike the rest of the crowd waiting to board the ferry to Provincetown on an unusually hot Boston day, the frail little man was covered from head to toe. A broad-brimmed Panama hat hid most of his face, followed by a khaki suit, and finally tan socks and handsome brown leather shoes. The shoes were so loose on his slender feet that they instantly conjured up the image of the much larger, stronger man he must have been before he met the illness that had left him with one, surely no more than two, months to live.

Elaine nudged Amanda, and for a moment, the two young women looked at the thin man with mingled curiosity and pity. Following their gaze, Larry glanced at him too, but with very different emotions. He felt, all over again, the cold sweat that had swept over him the week before, in the drab little waiting room of a clinic, while awaiting the results of a certain important test. And they had been negative. They had been negative.

As Larry absently watched the thin little man, some-thing in the tilt of the man's head, the exact angle of his hat brim, reminded him ... Larry brushed his muscular fore-arm, frosted with golden hair, across his face. He walked over to the chain fence that separated them from the blue water, where the ferry sat waiting for them.

"When will they let us on this damn boat?" he said under his breath.

A few minutes later, two ramps were lowered from the ferry's top deck, and the crowd began to push its way aboard.

The thin man got up, or, rather, unfolded, for he turned out to actually be very tall. He watched the crowd of vaca-tioners surge forward, standing with his hand on his hip as the harbor breeze tugged at his loose clothing. Clearly, he no longer saw the point of rushing. Amanda watched him, almost as if she expected him to say something to her, while her friends struggled, laughing, with their elaborate mess of beach chairs, tennis rackets, and suitcases. But the thin man simply drifted off, holding his hat carefully at a slight angle, like one who has long been in the habit of uncon-scious arrogance.

A long boat ride stretched ahead of the vacationers, a perfect time to begin a suntan or finish a novel. While the two women went below to buy a sandwich, Larry spread out his beach towel on the crowded top deck. The wide-open space quickly took on a party atmosphere as young men unrolled towels and blankets and stretched their near-naked bodies in the sun, talking and laughing and playing music on their transistor radios. Larry carefully applied suntan oil on his golden-haired chest, arms, and legs, at-tracting a few interested glances from the men around him. He put on his tape player headphones, lay down, and was soon fast asleep.

He woke up sweating; it had become intolerably hot. Now fully midday, the sun and sky and water had reached a scorching brightness. Larry sat up and murmured to the two women who were stretched out next to him that he was going to go below for a soda.

"Honey, would you put more lotion on my back?" Elaine asked. Larry obliged her, rubbing it gently into her olive skin, pursing his lips in an oddly maternal expression. He ended with a tickle under her arms.

"Would you like the same?" he asked Amanda, whose pale skin was already turning pink.

"No, thanks," she mumbled into her towel.

Elaine had known and adored him for years, but his charm had yet to capture Amanda, her new girlfriend. Larry was not overly concerned. He pulled on a fresh shirt and fished in his bag for a pack of cigarettes.

Down below, out of the sun, it was much more comfortable. A five-piece band was playing a very slow, lilting show tune, and several elderly women on a group tour were stepping about to the music. On his way past, Larry paused long enough to take one of them on a spin around the improvised dance floor. She smiled at him shyly, delighted, and her blue-haired friends all clapped.

Farther down the deck, Larry found a nice quiet spot at the railing, from which he could see the first faint outline of land, like a dark edge forming on the horizon. He lit a cigarette and, sucking the smoke in deeply, raked his hands through the tangles that the wind had made in his blond hair. Thinking of Elaine's and Amanda's prone and shiny bodies stretched out upstairs, he smiled.

Just then, he felt something as light as a dead leaf settle on his arm. He turned, startled. The thin man they had seen on the dock stood close, touching him. Looking up, Larry saw deeply into a face from which the flesh had fallen away, leaving only a slight flicker of life in eyes that must have once been irresistibly handsome. The look brought back, unavoidably now, a lover of a long-ago summer, a Broadway dancer named Paul Adair. Surely this man, standing so near that Larry could hear each labored breath, could not be Paul. Larry was overcome by a sudden terror that the ghostly man was going to embrace him, for their silent exchange of glances had the nakedness of two people who have just pulled away from a kiss.

"Pardon me." A quiet voice issued from the man's un-moving lips. "May I trouble you for a light?"

"I'm sorry, I haven't got one," Larry said quickly, reflex-ively taking a step back and causing the man's slender hand to slip from his arm. Then, realizing that his cigarette made his lie obvious, Larry turned scarlet.

"I see." The shadowed eyes under the hat brim regis-tered first pain and then, very faintly, amusement. "Larry, wasn't it? I suppose you're thinking that I've changed, Larry." The thin lips curved. "You haven't." He coughed, covering his mouth with a silk handkerchief. Then he soundlessly slid away. When Larry looked around again, the apparition had disappeared. After a moment, Larry felt a burning sensation at the tips of his fingers — his cigarette.

"Shit," Larry said. He tossed the cigarette into the sea.

✳

Half an hour later, when the boat's horn sounded, Larry had not moved. All around him, people were gathering their belongings and hurrying to the top deck. Again he felt a hand on his arm, but this time the touch was charged with energy. He turned to find Elaine's pretty face, already brown, grinning at him. Her teeth looked very white.

"Boy-watching again?" she teased. "We'd better get our asses in gear, pumpkin, or we'll have to wait an hour to get off this boat."

Provincetown looked slightly unreal, like a tinted pho-tograph of a toy village, in the unflinching sun. Walking down the pier leading into the town, the girls pointed at gray-shingled houses and sailboats.

"Look at the windsurfer," Elaine shouted. "There I go!"

"Just don't get yourself killed," Larry said, a bit absentmindedly. He was keeping an eye on a familiar Panama hat well ahead of them in the crowd yet clearly visible above the heads of the other tourists. When Larry's group reached the center of town, they would turn left, toward the west end. Just then, it seemed the most important thing in the world to Larry that the Panama hat not turn left as well. It was a long, hot walk to the end of the pier, even hotter when carrying, as Larry was, two suitcases as well as Elaine's golf clubs. The perspiration was dripping into his eyes. He watched with gradually increasing relief as the Panama hat slowly drifted over to the right side of the pier, turned right on the main street, and vanished.

At the lodgings, Larry took charge and got them settled in quickly. He had made all the arrangements, "Uncle Larry," as Elaine jokingly said. They were in a sunny little apartment overhanging the harbor. On the tiny balcony, pink geraniums planted in tubs tumbled about in the breeze.

"Even the bed's decent," said Amanda, flinging herself down.

"Larry, you're wonderful," Elaine said.

But Larry was already in his room, carefully unpacking his outfits for the week's vacation: seven casual shirts, three t-shirts, four pairs of good shorts, two pairs of cutoffs, two pairs of casual slacks, two bathing suits. He stripped off his soiled clothes quickly and dressed without his usual care. On his way out, he looked in on the girls. They were curled up together on the bed, already asleep. A peculiar look crossed Larry's face. Soundlessly, he let himself out of the apartment.

As the cocktail hour approached, people flooded out of their lodgings into the street. Most of the men moving toward and past and around Larry were young and brown and healthy, and many were also very handsome. Larry, as a good-looking man walking alone in the street, attracted some interested glances. He ducked into Sharkey's, one of his favorite bars in town, a tiny underground cafe done up in turquoise and pink. As usual, the lesbians were crowded around the bar. Larry chose a table in the back and ordered his favorite drink, a milk shake flavored with Kahlua. He felt an odd uneasiness, a sense of somehow being out of place, but reminded himself that he always felt that way at the beginning of a vacation.

Two dark men, perhaps ten years younger than Larry, watched him from a nearby table. They looked vaguely familiar — maybe he had met them at a party last summer? Finally, one of them, a stocky boy in a fishnet tank top, walked over.

"Weren't you on the Boston boat?"

"Today? Yes," said Larry.

"Want to join us?"

"Sure." After Larry sat down and introduced himself (using his first name only; he'd been at this longer than they had), he reached for a cigarette. But his fingertips still stung from the cigarette burn. Larry took another sip of his drink and smiled at the boys. "Your first season? My ninth, believe it or not. Maybe I could point you in the right direction."

"What about that club across the street?"

"That's strictly for the girls. But you must try the Flute, just two blocks down. Gorgeous decor, lovely view..."

"But where's the action?" the boy in the fishnet top wanted to know. "We're only here three days."

Larry's eyelids flickered briefly — a sign of disdain, had his companions known it — and then he smiled. "Try the Dominion, on the east end. Some leather, lots of fabulous boys."

"Keep on talking," the boy said, gesturing to the waiter.

"This round is on me," Larry said smoothly. "When you go to the beach, feel free to take your suit off, but watch out — rangers do patrol on horseback. Someone will warn you. One time years ago I fell asleep in the nude. I woke up with a man I'd never seen before shaking me and shouting, 'Ranger, ranger!' I thought: these New England boys are *very* forward."

Everyone laughed.

"Maybe we'll bump into you at the beach tomorrow," the stocky one said, "with or without your suit."

Larry smirked, showing his dimples. "Which would you prefer?"

"I'd prefer tonight," the boy countered boldly, but then he glanced nervously at his friend. "Why not?" he added, looking openly at Larry's well-muscled arms and chest. "You don't look sick to me." Seeing a slight change in Larry's expression, the boy quickly added, "You can't be too careful nowadays."

There was an unexpectedly long silence. Larry looked away, not at anybody in Sharkey's, but at some abstract and distant point. "But you can," he said softly. "You can be too careful." He got up awkwardly, dropped some money on the table, and pushed his chair into place. "Tired ... traveling ... sorry ... bump into you again," he muttered.

After he left, the two boys agreed that the "blond beauty" must have tested positive.

✳

That night, when the girls asked him to join them for dinner, Larry excused himself, saying that he was tired. He went to bed at ten o'clock, but he did not sleep. Again and again he relived his encounter with his dying friend, rewriting the exchange to make his part less shameful, inventing long conversations in which Paul told him about his suffering while he, Larry, listened and gave comfort.

He heard, dimly, as if from a great distance, the girls returning, moving stealthily so as not to wake him. But their presence did not comfort him. Larry felt that Paul alone held up the mirror in which he must look at himself forever.

The very next day, Larry's strange search began. Walking down the beach, his eyes combed the crowds of sunbathers for a frail and slender form, but all he found was an endless parade of bronzed and muscular men. Often, they returned his gaze as if expecting something more, but he looked past them, frowned, and kept on walking. The same happened in the bar that night: Larry fell into conversations easily but dropped out in midsentence, looking around every time the door opened and a new group of men walked in.

Each succeeding day was very much like the first one, only they slipped by faster and faster. Larry became increasingly restless, unable to remain still or to break away from his secret search. He even called the local hospital to ask if there was a patient named Adair. He walked up and down the main street, seeing little of the people or goods on display, but soothed by being in motion.

On the last day of his vacation, Larry was walking in the most crowded part of town when he saw something that made his heart jump. Three blocks up the street, where the crowd was thinner, a nun was pushing an invalid in a wheelchair. The thin figure was wrapped in shawls and almost blocked from view by the nun's black cape. But Larry caught a glimpse of a Panama hat.

His heart pounding, he pushed his way through the crowd. Young men walking hand in hand and families strolling five abreast cheerfully ignored his attempts to get past them. The wheelchair disappeared around a corner. Freeing himself of the crowd, Larry dashed around the corner and ran up the hill after the nun's flapping black cape.

"Please — please let me help you," he panted. The nun stopped and stared at him. Then the figure in the wheelchair turned. Under the wide hat brim was the plump, pouting face of an old lady, carefully rouged and lipsticked. Frowning, she tapped her cane on the sidewalk.

"We're in a hurry to get home," the nun said. "We appreciate your kindness, sir."

"I'm sorry," Larry said. "I'm really very sorry." He stepped back into the street without looking, and just missed being hit by a cyclist.

"What the fuck do you think you're doing!" the cyclist yelled.

On the ferry that afternoon, Larry stood in the stern and watched the town's gray shoreline slip away until there was nothing left to watch.

"We've lost sight of land!" a little girl cried out.

Larry felt the tears rise up from the deepest part of his insides, rolling up and through him and shaking his whole frame. He became aware, not by sight but somehow through his pores, of Elaine's warm presence beside him. He grabbed her and clung to her and wept like a child, forgetting, for the moment, everything but his need for comfort.

Elaine just held him quietly, not yet asking any questions, but deeply touched — and surprised. In ten years of friendship, she had never once seen Larry cry.

Michael Nava — Grief

Wearing plastic gloves, Nicholas Trejo, thirty-three, widow, knelt beside the toilet scrubbing the inside of the bowl with a scouring pad in an effort to erase the months-old ring of scum. Gradually, he restored the porcelain to a semblance of its original whiteness. Now he paused and sat back on his haunches, distracted by the thought that in cleaning the toilet he had probably expunged some last trace of Ed, a coil of reddish pubic hair, or urine stain, or fecal skid mark. The grayish water settled in the bowl, and he remembered the cloudiness in Ed's eyes just before he went blind.

The cause of Nick's spurt of domesticity had been a call three days earlier from his friend Jack Frey in San Francisco asking Nick if Jack's English cousin could stay with him.

"He's twenty-five," Jack said, "and he's traveling on his own, and he's broke."

"Look, Jack, it's just that..." Nick started to say.

"He's really a sweet kid, Nick. I'm sure he won't be any trouble. He's been here for a month, and I've hardly noticed him."

Nick twisted the phone cord between his fingers, picturing Jack at the other end of the line, hook-nosed, skinny, his darting eyebrows inflecting his conversation like accent marks. He had been Ed's lover before Nick. Upon meeting Nick for the first time, Jack had thrown a wiry arm around him and said, "Listen, doll, if you get into a jam with Miss Thing, give me a call. I know where the bodies are buried." Over the years Jack had been a good friend to both of them, and he'd been there at the end, on the day that Ed turned his blind eyes in Nick's direction and said, "It should have been you."

"I don't know, Jack, I'm working on a new book..." His voice trailed off. He hadn't put pen to paper in six months.

"Liar," Jack said mildly. "You told me yourself last time we talked that you haven't written anything more taxing than a grocery list in months. Now what's really going on?"

"I haven't had anyone over since Ed died."

"No one?" He could picture Jack's eyebrows creeping upward. "When was the last time you got laid?"

"I'm engaged to my VCR. Announcements to follow."

Jack laughed his barking laugh. "Listen, hon, if you're going to marry an appliance choose a vibrator."

"Yeah, I probably should," Nick said, "it's not easy getting a condom over a VCR. What about you?"

Jack made a sound that was a verbal shrug. "If it happens, it happens." Then he said, "So listen, put Rupert up for a couple of days, would you?"

Nick was inspecting the level of dust on the bookshelves. "Rupert?"

"My cousin, Rupert Smith. He's a law student, very smart and very nice, Nick. Really, I gave him one of your books, and he loved it."

"Appeals to my vanity..."

"Never fail — you're a writer," Jack said. "He'll be there Friday."

"He can stay as long as he promises not to track his tricks through the house."

Jack said, "He's got a boyfriend in London, and Rupert doesn't seem like the straying kind."

"Fine," Nick said, taking down a volume of his own work from the bookshelf.

"How are you doing on the Ed front?" Jack asked.

"Ed who?" Nick replied, opening the book.

"Okay, we'll talk again."

After they'd hung up, Nick looked at the dedication page. "For Ed," it said, "who hurt me into poetry."

"What, you into S&M?" someone had asked him upon reading this, not recognizing the crib from Auden. Ed, standing nearby, had glanced at Nick and smirked; he had warned Nick the allusion was too highbrow.

After he cleaned the shower, Nick pulled off his sweatpants and t-shirt, ran the water, and got in. As he soaped himself slowly, he could feel the growing softness of his body. Ed had almost persuaded Nick that the difference in their physiques was moral, not metabolic. At his goading, Nick had dieted and exercised until he acquired the same anonymous suit of muscles that everyone had. Now he was getting fat from lack of exercise and an indifferent diet, fulfilling what he thought of as his physiognomical destiny. What had been pecs were now becoming titties. Nostalgically, he pictured himself turning into his grandmother, his *abuelita*, a squat, big-breasted woman tending an ever-simmering pot of beans, her apron pockets full of hard candy.

Showered and dressed, he poured himself a glass of wine and went into the living room to await his houseguest. The room was L-shaped, the shorter space serving as a dining area. From the living room, a sliding door opened onto a narrow patio furnished with a couple of wicker chairs. In the dining room were floor-to-ceiling windows. Interior shutters usually covered both door and windows, but today Nick had pulled the shutters back.

His apartment was on the third floor of a three-story building, level with the tops of trees that lined the quiet West Hollywood street below. Looking out upon the tree-tops and the late afternoon sky, Nick thought, for the whatever-thousandth time, that it was like living in a tree house. Our castle in the sky, Ed called it, which, depending on his inflection and his mood, could sound like a line out of either *Mary Poppins* or *Who's Afraid of Virginia Woolf?* Nick sipped from the wineglass. Cold and dry, the wine stung at first and then, as it warmed in his mouth, went bland as spit. He swallowed, and it left no aftertaste.

He had hoped that death would provide a kind of statute of limitations on his feelings about Ed. Dying had turned Ed into the monster Nick had always suspected lay not far beneath the polished surface, a monster of fear and selfishness. He had struck out savagely with his dwindling power as if the ability to cause pain confirmed that he was still alive. Nick had taken most of it. In his rage he willed Ed to die, and when Ed did, Nick was left with the inevitable emotional consequences.

He had not slept for weeks after Ed's death, and he had often ended up on the patio, drink in hand, feeling contaminated by death. When this wore off, he felt a depression so dense he thought he must be physically sick. But that came later, the spate of minor illnesses and infections like a cruel parody of Ed's afflictions. And then it all stopped. He had awakened one morning healthy, functional, and harrowed. Diminished, he went about the small activities that made up his life.

✳

The phone rang. Nick answered. "Hello."

"Nick? This is Rupert Smith. Jack Frey's cousin."

"Are you downstairs?"

"Yes, I am."

"I'll buzz you in. I'm in 318." It occurred to Nick his guest might need a hand bringing up his luggage. He got up and found a pair of shoes, but by the time he'd put them on Rupert was knocking at the door.

❋

"Nick? Hi. I'm Rupert." Rupert, a tall, dark-haired boy, put out his hand as he spoke, causing his canvas shoulder bag to slide down his arm. Hastily he withdrew the outstretched hand and caught the bag before it slipped to the floor, muttering through a smile, "Sorry."

"Here, give it to me." Nick took the wayward bag, brushing the boy's hand in the process. "Come in."

An instant's uncertainty flickered across the boy's face. Nick caught his eye and smiled recognition of the awkwardness of the moment.

"Please," he said, standing aside to let Rupert in. "Welcome. How's Jack?"

Invoking Jack put the boy at ease. Decisively, he picked up the suitcase that rested against a long leg and stepped into the room. "He's fine. He sends his love."

"Let's put your stuff in the living room for now," Nick said, leading the boy inside and closing the door behind him. Rupert dropped his suitcase against the wall and walked to the edge of the black-and-gold Oriental carpet in the center of the room.

"This is lovely," Rupert said. Nick followed his glance as he took in the room's furnishings: the glove-soft Italian leather sofas; the glass-topped coffee tables on pedestals of twisted steel, one surmounted by a glass vase holding red and yellow tulips and the other by a ceramic bowl in which a half-dozen gardenias floated; a spectral lamp that seemed more a sculpture than a lighting fixture; the rosewood bookshelves; and various other carefully chosen clutter. "It looks right out of a magazine."

"It was," Nick said. "My lover was an interior designer. This was his laboratory, sort of."

"Oh, yes, your lover. Edward?" Rupert said, his tone appropriately hushed. "Jack told me he died. I'm so sorry."

"Ed," Nick replied, out of habit, then explained, "He insisted on being called Ed. He said it sounded less like a fag decorator that way. Can I get you a drink?"

Rupert sat down, picked up Nick's wineglass, and smiled charmingly. "Whatever you're having."

"I'll take that," Nick said, reaching for the glass. "Make yourself at home. Play some music, if you like," he added, disappearing into the kitchen. A moment later he heard Ella Fitzgerald singing Cole Porter.

Nick set down the bottle of wine to listen. Officially, Ed had deplored Nick's taste in music; "pre-Stonewall," he called it, preferring whatever was up-to-the-minute at the bars. Hearing Ella sing "Skylark" made him think of Ed sitting glumly on the sofa, martini in hand, rolling his eyes.

"You're such a faggot," Ed would say.

To which Nick replied, "That doesn't seem to bother you in bed," when they were sleeping together and, "Get her," when they weren't. Half a drink later, Ed would be humming along.

Nick drew a deep breath, poured chardonnay into two tall glasses, added a splash of cassis and a twist of lemon rind. He put the drinks on a tray, emptied a can of mixed nuts into a glass bowl, added this to the tray, and carried it into the living room wondering if he would ever know anyone as well as he had known Ed.

"Cocktails," he announced.

Rupert watched wide-eyed as Nick settled the tray on the coffee table. "Oh, superb," he said, taking a glass. "A kir."

Nick took his glass and sat down across from Rupert. "Excellent choice of music. *Salud*."

"Cheers," Rupert said, his eyes never leaving Nick's face.

The tape ran on from one romantic song to the next, and Nick found himself taking Rupert in. At first glance, Rupert had seemed ordinarily nice-looking, good skin, smooth hair, regular features. A closer look revealed attractive asymmetries. The corners of his eyes turned down rather cruelly, but his eyes were without guile. The ragged hairline was endearing, but his big slab of mouth was all sex, and there was something of a wince in his broadest smile. He picked the lemon rind out of his drink and chewed it, then licked his stubby fingers for the taste of lemon. Until that moment, Nick's assessment had been more aesthetic than sexual, but watching the boy's earnest mastication, he wondered how he would be in bed. From Rupert's appraising glance he surmised that similar speculation was also running through Rupert's head. Their eyes met briefly, confirming their mutual interest.

Gulping the last of his drink, Rupert said, "You're Spanish?"

"Mexican," Nick said, adding "-American. And you're English."

"Oh, the accent gave me away did it?"

Nick said, "More the idiom than the accent. I have an English friend who sounds just like you except that all her locutions are strictly American."

"I must meet her," Rupert insisted. "She can teach me to talk like a Californian."

Nick said, "That's not as easy as it sounds. Californians don't have a distinctive accent."

"You do to me," Rupert said. "You sound like a boy from university on whom I had the most unrequited crush. His people were from here, I think. Is there a place called Tarzania?"

"In Africa," Nick said. "You mean Tarzana. Named for Tarzan."

213

"Really? That's it, I'm sure." He grabbed a handful of nuts from the bowl before him and stuffed them into his mouth. "You don't look like him, though."

"Look like who?" Nick asked.

"My would-be honey," Rupert replied, swallowing and looking regretfully at his empty glass. "He was a surfer. You look more like a priest."

"I think you mean nun," Nick replied and nudged his glass across the table. "Here, finish mine, and I'll make us both another."

"Thanks," Rupert said, taking the glass. "And, no, not a nun. You look like one of those dark-haired Italian curates whom altar boys dream of being seduced by."

Nick leaned toward him slightly and asked, "Were you ever an altar boy?"

"I just have an active fantasy life," Rupert replied, smiling over the rim of the glass. He took a swallow and set the glass down, licking the corner of his mouth.

"Your lover shares it, I hope."

"Charley's long-suffering," he laughed. He rooted through the nuts for the cashews. "You're much handsomer than the pictures of you in your books."

"Thank you," Nick said, inclining his head in a jokey bow. "You're quite good-looking, too." He grinned. "Are you flirting with me, by the way? Jack said you were happily married."

Rupert went faintly red in the face, but his voice was unembarrassed. "I'm on holiday."

"You and Charley have an understanding?"

"Well..." Rupert said, picking the lemon rind out of Nick's glass. "I suppose you could call it *de facto* rather than *de jure.*"

"That sounds like law school Latin for 'no' to me," Nick said, rising. "I'll get us another round. How long have you been traveling, by the way?"

214

"Eight weeks. The longest I've been away from England."

"You miss him?"

"I guess that depends," Rupert replied, with a wide, pained smile.

✳

After an hour, and two more drinks, Nick suggested dinner before they got drunk. Risibly high, they walked to a nearby deli. Over bagels and lox and Mexican beer Rupert recounted his adventures in America. He was, Nick thought, a sunny child but not half the naïf he pretended to be. Eventually the conversation drifted to Nick.

"Jack gave me one of your books to read," Rupert said, "the one called *Student*. I liked it quite a lot."

"Bless you," Nick replied, pouring the last of his beer into his glass. "It sold three copies, I think."

"Oh," Rupert said, nonplussed, "but you live so well."

A waitress cleared their dishes. "Ed supported me," Nick said crisply, "and some of the other books did make money." He ordered coffee. "Still not enough to live on but," he shrugged, "Ed left me everything."

He was aware that as he'd spoken his voice had acquired the faintly disparaging tone it always took on when he talked about Ed. He hoped Rupert hadn't noticed.

"He believed in you. As a writer, I mean," Rupert said, drawing the sentimental conclusion.

Nick knew he should reply with equal sentimentality but instead he said, "No, he just liked playing patron of the arts. The only use he had for books was as decoration."

"It doesn't seem that you got along very well," Rupert said, in a tone inviting Nick to contradict him.

But the familiar demons had taken over. His rage at Ed — or Ed's death — always so close to the surface, erupted. "No," he said, spilling sugar into his coffee, "we didn't."

"Then why did you continue on?"

"I don't know. Why do you stay with your boyfriend?"

"I love him," Rupert said.

"Well, that wasn't why I stayed with Ed," Nick replied dismissively. "It was just less trouble to stay than to go until he got sick and then there was no going — for me, I mean."

"I can't believe that," Rupert said, sounding really hurt.

"You should be relieved that I'm not sentimental."

"What do you mean?"

"It'll make it easier for you to sleep with me."

"I'm not sure that would be right," Rupert said stiffly.

"Whatever," Nick replied and called for the check.

❋

The walk home was as silent as the walk to the restaurant had been voluble. Nick didn't know how to explain to Rupert that Ed's death had robbed him of the chance to resolve their difficult relationship face-to-face and condemned him to quarrel with a ghost. He only knew he regretted his outburst, but he was afraid that Rupert would take his apology as a sexual ploy, so he said nothing. Rupert was absorbed in his own silence.

Suddenly, Rupert turned and said, "I wonder — please don't think I'm a sod — but could we go to a bar?"

"A gay bar?"

"Yes," Rupert said. "I'd like to see what they're like here."

"As compared to San Francisco?" Nick asked. "Or didn't Jack take you around?"

"He doesn't drink, you know."

"Oh, that's right. He's on the wagon. Sure, why not," he said, welcoming the diversion. "We'll just get my car and I'll give you a quick tour."

216

*

The first place they went to was a video bar. Entering the hushed blue room, Nick saw a couple of dozen of men, drinks in hand, staring adamantly at the video screens posted in the bar's four corners. Pee Wee Herman segued into "I Love Lucy" and then an old Cyndi Lauper video.

"Not very convivial" was Rupert's comment.

"Ed used to call it 'The Petrified Forest.'"

Rupert's smile was questioning.

Nick explained the allusion and added, "It was also the name of an old Humphrey Bogart movie."

"Oh, I see. Do you want a drink?"

"A brandy, maybe."

They found a perch on a long bench against the wall and sat side by side. Nick watched the men watching the videos, saw how they'd sneak side glances at one another from time to time, or walk the few steps from one end of the room to the other, shift position, try on a different attitude. It had been a long time since he'd been at a bar. He felt as if he had returned to a place where he had once lived and thought he'd passed for a native, only now to discover that he had probably fooled no one. Had he not met Ed at a business lunch, he wondered if he would ever have found anyone at all. An image passed through his head of the first time he'd seen Ed, a tall, slender redhead with amused green eyes, and it left him desolate.

"Did you and Ed go out to bars, then?"

"What?"

Rupert was tapping his foot and swaying slightly to the Janet Jackson song blaring overhead.

"You said Ed called this the Petrified Forest. Did you come here often?"

Nick shook his head. "Ed came. I read matchbook covers."

"I beg your pardon?"

"Ed liked having adventures. I preferred to make them up in stories."

"You weren't monogamous?"

"I was," Nick replied, "but not out of virtue. It was the logistics of carrying on that defeated me."

Rupert rubbed a long thumb back and forth across the back of Nick's hand. "Perhaps if you'd traveled..."

Nick was startled that Rupert was still interested but flattered, too. He mustered a suggestive smile. "Seen enough of the bars for tonight?"

"Yes, let's go home."

＊

On the drive home, Nick massaged the boy's thigh, but when Rupert's muscles tensed in response, Nick removed his hand. The temperature in the car seemed to shift from moment to moment as Rupert debated with himself whether to go through with it. As for Nick, he was equally ambivalent but for different reasons. He'd hadn't had sex with anyone since Ed's death and only now, with the prospect before him, did the two things seem disturbingly connected.

He parked the car and they rode the elevator up in silence. Nick clicked on a light as they entered the apartment and headed for Rupert's suitcase, which still lay against the living room wall. Rupert hung back, uncertainly, and Nick, tired of waiting for Rupert to make his mind up, decided for him.

"I'll show you the spare room," he said, reaching for the suitcase.

He felt Rupert's hand caress the back of his neck. "I thought I'd sleep in your room," he said.

Nick straightened himself, but the boy's hand stayed where it was, massaging his neck. The blunt warm fingers prodded his muscles. He shut his eyes. "Are you sure?"

"Yes, quite," Rupert replied.

Turning to him, Nick said, "Okay," not knowing whether it was or not. They kissed. Rupert's tongue spurted into his mouth and Nick thought, oh, slam-bam-thank-you-Sam; good thing he wasn't sentimental.

✳

Rupert sweated heavily and his sweat seemed to activate the cologne of which Nick had barely been aware earlier in the evening. Now, the fragrance drenched the sheets, earth, darkly floral, like dusk would smell if it had a scent.

At this moment, the boy knelt above Nick, masturbating, while at the same time rubbing the crack of his ass back and forth across the tip of Nick's cock, which Nick obligingly held in place with one hand. With the other hand, he stroked Rupert's sweat-slicked thighs and chest, marveling at the seamless skin that passed beneath his fingertips. In the scented semi-darkness — the lamp had been left on low — Rupert was beautiful. He tilted back his head, uttered a kind of a coo, and sprayed semen across Nick's chest. A few drops splattered Nick's face as he fell back into the bed. He collected them with the edge of his finger and they formed a single drop that hung like a pearl from his fingertip before it dropped to his chest. He sniffed from his fingers the almost-forgotten smell of another man's semen.

Rupert sat back onto Nick's crotch, flattening his already subsiding hard-on, and smiled. "Mmm."

"You worked hard for that," Nick said, stroking Rupert's thighs with both hands.

"But you didn't come," Rupert said, reaching between his thighs for Nick's cock.

"Not necessary," Nick muttered. "You're really beautiful."

Rupert grinned painfully. "I think we need a towel here," he said quickly rising from the bed.

Aware that he'd overstepped some line that Rupert had drawn between them, Nick was at once annoyed and sorry. He wanted to say, "But you *are* beautiful." Instead, he watched the gobs of the boy's semen thin and begin to run down his chest and the sides of his torso. It made him sad, how the passion ended in little pools of dampness on the sheets and misunderstandings. Then it merely seemed ridiculous and he could dismiss the sadness, but still, some part of the feeling, some little grief, stayed in his body. He drew his fingers across his chest and wondered how much grief was already stored there.

✳

"I've never cheated on Charley before," Rupert said, giving himself a last wipe with the towel and tossing it to the floor. "Oops. I suppose you're the last one to whom I should be making these errant-husband noises."

"Do you feel guilty?"

"A little," he said. Dropping his head back onto the pillow, he added, "A lot, actually."

Nick stroked Rupert's still-stiffish cock. "This isn't the organ that one cheats with."

After a moment, Rupert said, "I thought you weren't sentimental."

"No, but I know something about cheating."

"Well, it's true that I'm not in love with you or anything like that," he said, "but you're not just the first convenient body, you know. There could have been others."

Nick made a noise he hoped was appreciative, but his head was busy with the echoing phrase, *not in love,* and he wondered why it hurt so much.

Patting Nick's shoulder, Rupert said, "Could you turn off the light?"

Nick switched off the lamp and eased himself into bed, his body touching Rupert's haphazardly, a thigh here, a foot there, and a hand briefly over a hand. Rupert made a swift movement and Nick found himself peering through the darkness at the boy's face above him.

"Goodnight, Nick," he whispered and kissed him sweetly on the lips. "Thank you."

Nick said, "Goodnight, Rupert. Sleep well."

✳

He woke up, his chest and stomach pasted to Rupert's back by sweat. Their bodies didn't fit together well. Nick's chin lay awkwardly in the boy's clavicle and his right arm was asleep beneath his own weight. His other arm was thrown across Rupert's chest and Rupert grasped his wrist. He felt the thud of Rupert's heart beneath his palm. Slowly, he extricated himself, until he was lying on his back staring at the ceiling. He and Ed had fit. They had held each other spoon style, even after they'd stopped having sex, on the good nights, when they'd fallen asleep friends.

On the other side of the bed, Rupert stirred and began to snore. Nick felt his chest constrict. Quietly, he got out of bed and went into the living room. By the time he had pulled back the shutters and slid open the door to the patio, the impulse to cry had passed.

✳

He stepped out onto the patio. The night was warmish still, and past the blaze of streetlights the flat, black sky unfolded without stars and without mystery. One night, not long after Ed's death, he'd been standing here when someone passed on the street below, playing a guitar, the clear notes sharp and sudden and distinct, but not quite music. Ed had had qualities that Nick loved, but they had not quite added up to a lovable man. Still, Ed had let Nick know him, had revealed himself, which, Nick realized, had taken remarkable courage. He, at least, had been willing to be loved or not loved. It was Nick, the fan of soppy ballads, the poet, who had held back, who had concealed himself.

Now he said, "I'm sorry."

He heard creaking in the bedroom, followed by shuffling footsteps and then a drowsy, "Nick?" Like an overgrown infant, Rupert stood naked at the doorway, yawning and rubbing his eyes. "Did my snoring wake you?"

"No," Nick replied. "Go to bed."

Sitting down on the sofa Rupert said, "I reckoned you'd gone to pee but when you didn't come back I got worried."

Stepping into the room, Nick said, "I'm all right."

"What woke you then?"

"I'm not sure," Nick replied sitting beside the boy. He put his arm around him.

Sleepily, Rupert leaned his head against Nick's and asked, "Can I do anything?"

Nick closed his eyes against his tears, pressed his fingers into the boy's warm flesh, and said, "This is fine for now."

The contributors

John Barrow grew up in Cordele, Georgia, and attended Emory University. His fiction has appeared in *Christopher Street*, and his plays have been staged by Trinity Theater and Stonewall Rep in New York, where he makes his home.

Randy Boyd is a writer of fiction and nonfiction living in the Los Angeles area. He is currently at work on a novel and a collection of short stories.

Jameson Currier's short fiction and essays have appeared in the *Crescent Review, Gulf Stream,* the *New York Native, Au Courant,* and *In Touch for Men.* He currently resides in New York City, and is at work on a collection of short stories.

Lucas Dedrick is a writer and student living in San Francisco. His stories have been published in the *James White Review* and in the anthology *The Gay Nineties,* published by Crossing Press.

Larry Duplechan is the celebrated author of the novels *Eight Days a Week* (Alyson), *Blackbird,* and *Tangled up in Blue* (St. Martin's). He lives in Los Angeles and is at work on his fourth novel.

Robert Friedman has contributed to the *San Francisco Sentinel, Lambda Book Report,* and *Painted Bride Quarterly.* Currently, he lives at the Radical Faerie Sanctuary in Wolf Creek, Oregon, where he is working on a novel.

Patrick D. Hoctel is the assistant editor of the *Bay Area Reporter* in San Francisco. His short fiction has appeared in *Men on Men* 1, the *James White Review, Christopher Street,* and *Tribe.*

Thomas Losito is a painter and a poet living in Albuquerque, New Mexico. He has previously been published in *Invert,* a poetry journal based in Connecticut. He makes his fiction debut with his contribution to this anthology.

Kelly McQuain is a writer and artist whose fiction has appeared in the *James White Review.* He recently received a master's degree in creative writing from Temple University, and makes his home in Philadelphia.

Anthony D. Miller lives and writes in Cumberland, Maryland.

Michael Nava is the author of three mystery novels, the most recent of which was *Howtown*. He is also the editor of *Finale*, an anthology of short mysteries published by Alyson Publications.

Lev Raphael's fiction has appeared in a wide range of publications including *Christopher Street*, *Redbook*, the *James White Review*, and *Hadassah*. He is also the author of the recent collection *Dancing on Tisha B'Av*, in which "Another Life" originally appeared.

Guillermo Reyes recently completed an MFA in playwriting at UC San Diego. His story "Lorca's Curse" was originally published in *Christopher Street*, and other works have appeared in the *Americas Review* and *Shadows of Love*, a short-fiction anthology published by Alyson.

Michael Schwartz is the author of a media watch column for the *Front Page*, a gay and lesbian newspaper based in Raleigh, North Carolina. This is his first published fiction. He lives in Boston with his lover, Jeff Knudsen.

David Watmough is a thirty-year resident of Vancouver, British Columbia. He has just completed his tenth book about his ongoing gay protagonist, Davey Bryant. Some of his previous novels are *No More into the Garden, Families,* and *The Year of Fears.*

Carter Wilson's fourth novel, *Treasures on Earth*, was reissued by Alyson in 1990. His stories, articles, and reviews have appeared in the *Advocate, Christopher Street,* and the *Lavender Reader.* Wilson also worked on the narration for two Academy Award–winning documentaries, *The Times of Harvey Milk* and *Common Threads.*

Virginia Witt is currently at work on a collection of short stories about the lives of gays and lesbians. She has been writing in various genres for more than fifteen years, and lives with her partner in Washington, D.C.

Ron Woewoda is a writer living and working in Powell River, British Columbia.